A Case of Suicide in St. James's

A Freddy Pilkington-Soames Adventure Book 5

Clara Benson

Mount Street Press

Mount Street Press

Copyright

ISBN: 978-1-913355-14-2

ClaraBenson.com

Cover design by Shayne Rutherford at wickedgoodbookcovers.com

Interior Design & Typesetting by Ampersand Book Interiors
ampersandbookinteriors.com

FROM THE *CLARION* OF
THURSDAY, 19TH OF JUNE, 1930

Lady Browncliffe is to give a dance for her daughter, the Hon. Patricia Nugent, at her home in St. James's Square this evening. The Artie Squires band is engaged to play, and an al fresco supper will be served in the garden. It was recently announced that Miss Nugent is to marry Thomas Chetwynd, the son of Air Chief Marshal Sir Thomas Bryce Chetwynd, Chief of the Air Staff.

CHAPTER ONE

IT WAS TWO o'clock on a slow afternoon in the middle of June, and Fleet Street was drooping in the heat. The ground was parched and glaring, the buildings dusty and the smells unsavoury. Motor-cars practically coughed in the dry air, while horses limped along instead of trotting, their heads flopping forward and their coats gleaming with perspiration. Everywhere windows had been thrown wide open—although it was doubtful if this was of utility to anyone except burglars, since there was not a breath of a breeze to be felt. After an interminably chilly spring, summer had arrived with a vengeance, and those who had complained most vociferously of the cold were now afforded the pleasure of complaining about the heat instead.

In the offices of the *Clarion*, that beacon of truth and righteousness, half the employees had either managed to wangle themselves some time off, or resorted to underhand methods to ensure they were given stories about society picnics and children's charabanc trips to the sea, that they might escape the stuffy indoors and enjoy the glorious sunshine. Not so Freddy Pilkington-Soames, who had essayed a gambit which had not paid off, having, during the previous week's torrential rain, ruthlessly cheated a fellow-reporter in order to obtain a story which would keep him indoors. Unfortunately, the story in question, involving a long-standing feud between two rival Chambers of Commerce, which had begun over a minor matter of policy and had descended into finger-pointing and name-calling between grown men who ought to have known better, quickly proved to be so insufferably tedious that Freddy had ever since bitterly regretted not taking the lawn tennis assignment instead—especially since the weather had almost immediately cleared up, and his bested colleague was now spending each afternoon enjoying the hospitality of the All-England Club and returning to the office every evening in a cheerfully well-oiled condition. In addition to this patently inequitable state of affairs, Freddy had also been saddled with the task of compiling the paper's Social Diary, since the girl who usually did it had gone on holiday, leaving the job to him with what he considered to be unduly malicious glee. The assignment was not in itself unpleasant, but he had in the course of his duties discovered one or two fashionable social events to which he had unaccountably not been invited—including a party thrown by his own mother—which put him in a worse mood than before. The heat was stifling and the work exasperating, and to top it all he had a ringing headache which was entirely his own doing, caused as it was by his unwise decision to stay out drinking until four o'clock that morning.

The day was not going well, and the air showed no signs of cooling. Freddy reached over to push at the window, although it was already almost as far open as it would go. He glanced around, and found that his section of the news-room was almost deserted. He threw down his pencil. It was too hot to work, and he was feeling the soporific effects of a large lunch; surely it could do no harm to take forty winks? He leaned back in his chair and put his feet up on the desk in front of him, closed his eyes gently, felt the heat surround him like a caress, and prepared to be comfortable.

He was rudely interrupted in his preparations by a female voice, which was at once familiar and impossible to ignore.

'So this is what you do all day, is it?' it said, and before he could collect his thoughts he felt his feet being pushed sideways off the desk, to land on the floor with a thump. He opened his eyes and sat up in some indignation, and saw before him, sitting on the desk in the exact spot his feet had formerly occupied, Gertie McAloon, second daughter of the Earl of Strathmerrick. She was wearing a wisp of a frock which floated like gossamer, would certainly not stand up to vigorous washing, and had no doubt cost an enormous amount of money, and she looked as cool and fresh as an early spring day.

'Hallo, beast,' she said amiably.

'What are you doing here?' he said. 'Oughtn't you to be at your family stronghold in the North just now, rampaging through the heather and striking mortal terror into the hearts of the Scots?'

'Not this year. After the floods last winter half the East wing collapsed, and they're still digging people out. The works won't be finished until next year,' said Gertie. 'It's a dreadful bore, but Father says the insurance won't cover the work so we can't afford to go anywhere else. I suggested he try and make up the difference at roulette, since at least that way we'd get a week in Monte Carlo, but he didn't seem to think much of the idea, so here I am, still in London.'

'So you are.'

'You might make an effort to be happy to see me. You're looking awfully glum.'

'Wouldn't you be in my position?' said Freddy. '*You* can leave this infernal building whenever you want. I have to stay here until six and pretend to work.'

'Poor you! Yes, I expect it is rather beastly. We must find a way to cheer you up. I know—let's have a wild affair!' she suggested brightly.

'My dear girl, I'm absolutely stony at the moment and couldn't possibly afford you,' said Freddy. 'And besides, haven't we already tried that?'

'Have we?' she said blankly.

'Yes, don't you remember? It was last summer at that ridiculous do at what's-her-name's—Priss's friend and her ghastly husband. It lasted about two days.'

'Oh, was that you?' said Gertie. 'I thought it was Mungo.'

'Did you? It was obviously very memorable, then.'

'It was profoundly unsatisfactory, as I recall. Tremendously dull. Hardly worth bothering, in fact.'

'If this is your attempt at cheering me up it's failing signally,' said Freddy pointedly.

'Yes, but—look here, are you sure it wasn't Mungo?'

'Not unless you were carrying on with him at the same time. Not that I'd put it past you, but since he was in Baden-Baden all last summer, I should say it's unlikely.'

'Oh,' said Gertie, disconcerted. 'Well, then, never mind, we'll forget that. But you'll still be my bodyguard at this party tonight, won't you?'

'Which party? What are you talking about?'

'Tatty Nugent's, of course. That's why I'm here. She's just got engaged to the Chetwynd boy and they'll be sailing about together looking fearfully smug because she swiped him from me quite shamelessly, and it won't do at all to let her think she's won, especially since I ended it all with Douglas. I only got engaged to *him* as a sort of revenge, but it would never have worked, and after a week I began to feel rather stupid and thought I'd let him go gently, but he took it badly, which is absurd because I was sure he'd only asked me on the rebound, but he got awfully grumpy, and now he looks daggers at me and makes pointed remarks whenever I see him, and he'll be there tonight making me feel uncomfortable, so I need someone to protect me, which is why I thought of you.'

'I think you must be speaking Norwegian, because I didn't understand a word of that,' said Freddy. 'Have you been getting engaged again? How many times is that now? The *Clarion* gives discounts for multiple advertisements, you know.'

'Don't be impudent. This is only the fourth—well, that's not counting Johnny Peverell, but there wasn't time for an engagement as such there, so I suppose you'd call that one an elopement, and Father had it annulled anyway, which was all for the best, I dare say, even if he was astonishingly good-looking, as he really didn't know how to hold his fork properly and his vowels were frankly appalling.'

'Johnny Peverell? The racing-driver? Why didn't I know about that?'

'It was quite the least interesting thing I did last year,' said Gertie airily. 'But never mind that. Are you coming or not? You are invited, I take it?'

'Yes, but I was thinking of giving it a miss.'

'Whatever for? That's not like you. Are you sickening for something?'

'No, I—' began Freddy, but got no further before there was an interruption in the form of Jolliffe, a fellow-reporter of Freddy's, who had been out all morning.

'Freddy, why aren't you outside in this glorious weather?' he said as he came in. 'I've been watching the "Birtles' Bathing Beauties" contest by the boating lake in Regent's Park. They're all delightful-looking girls, I must say, and they were looking very fetching in their bathing things.'

Freddy, who had spent the morning listening respectfully to elderly gentlemen in a stuffy room while sitting on a hard chair, glared. Jolliffe did not notice, and went on:

'I'd have been back earlier, but I had to stay and talk to some of the witnesses. It'll make quite a nice little story, I dare say, and Mr. Bickerstaffe will be pleased the *Clarion* was there to catch it and get one up on the *Herald*.'

'Witnesses? What witnesses?'

'Oh, it was that ass Corky Beckwith. He decided to try and jazz the story up a bit, but ended up being the story himself!' Jolliffe began to laugh. 'He pretended to trip while he was passing the line of girls and shoved about five of them in the lake. I think the idea was that he'd dive in and rescue them, but it was as clear as daylight that he'd done it on purpose, and as it turned out they could all swim anyway. He did his best—jumped in and got hold of one of them, but she was having none of it and socked him one on the jaw. Then all five of them turned on him and held him under, and if it hadn't been for a passing bobby I expect they'd have drowned him. How we all hooted! Such a shame you missed all the fun.'

It was indeed. Freddy would have given a not inconsiderable amount of money to have witnessed the spectacle of Corky Beckwith making a fool of himself, and was about to say so sourly when Jolliffe spotted Gertie and said:

'Hallo, Gertie, I didn't realize you were here.'

'Hallo, Reggie,' said Gertie. 'So this where all the young men of London spend their days, is it? Funny, I had no idea so many people had to work for a living. I'm just trying to persuade Freddy to come to Tatty's party. Do be a sport, Freddy. If you won't I'll have to ask Reggie. You wouldn't mind, would you, Reggie?'

'Er—' began Jolliffe.

'And that would never do,' she went on. 'He's far too tame. Look at him—he'll be demanding cocoa and falling asleep by ten o'clock.'

'I say,' protested Jolliffe mildly.

'Oh very well,' said Freddy, who was not about to stand for the indignity of being rejected in favour of Jolliffe. 'We can go together if you like, and I'll protect you from this—what's he called again?'

'Douglas Westray, his name is.'

'Westray? Any relation to Sir Stanley Westray, the aeroplane manufacturer?'

'It's his son.'

'And you got engaged to him to make Tatty Nugent jealous but ditched him almost immediately because you realized you didn't care for him in the slightest?'

'More or less,' admitted Gertie. 'Doug and Tatty were rather the thing for a while, but then she decided Tom Chetwynd was a better prospect, even though she knew I'd had a crush on him for simply months. I'm sure Tom doesn't care a ha'penny for her, but he'd got himself tangled up with some unsuitable girl, and his pa threatened to disinherit him if he didn't get rid of her then pushed him into marrying Tatty instead. Doug was pretty cut up about the whole thing—he and Tom have been the best of friends practically since birth—and I felt sorry for him and wanted to annoy Tatty, so I thought it couldn't do any harm. But it would never have worked. He's handsome in a brooding sort of way, but no fun at all. So I gave him the boot after a week.'

'I don't suppose that made him feel any better.'

'No, it didn't—although you'd think it would have, since it was perfectly obvious we weren't suited.'

'So am I to expect that he'll be in a foul temper and wanting to punch somebody? By whom I mean me?'

'I shouldn't think so,' said Gertie. 'He's not the type—and besides, he was only invited on condition that he promised to behave like a gentleman and not cause trouble. He'll probably just hang around like a bad smell, gazing mournfully at us and ruining the mood.'

'Isn't he more likely to hang around Tatty, if he was in love with her?'

'Now there's a thought,' said Gertie, brightening. 'Do you know, I shouldn't be surprised if he did. I do hope you're right, then I can watch the spectacle from afar and enjoy it.'

'Full of the milk of human kindness, aren't you?'

'What are you talking about?' said Gertie vaguely. She slid down from the desk. 'All right then, I'd better be off. I'll be there about eight. Dress decently so I won't be ashamed to be seen with you. You're handsome enough in a dim light. Sir Stanley and Lois Westray are bringing me, to keep me out of trouble, Mother says, although you'd think she'd have given up trying by now in the face of the evidence.'

'Isn't your mother coming?'

'No, she's taking Priss to some do or other—which reminds me: she said to ask you to lunch on Sunday, as she hasn't seen you for ages.'

'But I thought she didn't like me. I'm pretty sure your father doesn't, at any rate.'

'Oh, don't worry about him—he's up at Fives, living in a cottage and supervising the work. It's a good thing, really, as it means I won't have to tell him about Douglas. He's started going slightly green in the face every time I announce my engagement.'

'I'm not surprised,' muttered Freddy, as Gertie went out.

Chapter Two

THE EVENING-PARTY thrown for Miss Patricia Nugent by her mother, Lady Browncliffe, took place at the family's London abode, Badenoch House, one of the grandest establishments in St. James's Square. The house, as befitted the wealth of its owner, Lord Browncliffe (formerly Walter Nugent of the Nugent Corporation), was a tall, stately building in grey brick, with steps leading up to a magnificent double front door in gleaming black (presently flung wide open), which led through a vestibule into an entrance-hall with black and white floor tiles of polished marble so smooth that there was great danger of slipping on them if care was not taken. Inside, the first thing that met the eye was an enormous chandelier which hung from a ceiling that was at least forty feet from the ground, made up of hundreds if not thousands of pear-shaped drops of highly-polished crystal, which glittered and twinkled merrily, stirred by the movement of the many people milling about in the hall below, for there was very little breeze. All the public rooms of the house were bedecked from top to bottom with luscious blooms of pink roses and spiky white gladioli, which filled the stifling air with heavy perfume. The dancing was taking place in the ballroom to the left of the grand staircase, a sombre-looking room, all dark panelling and mauve wallpaper, which was doing its best to look cheerful with the addition of several dozen electric lamps and the presence of a lively jazz orchestra playing with determined energy at the far end. Two sets of French windows had been thrown open, alleviating the closeness of the air only slightly, but in spite of the heat a good number of revellers—mostly those who had consumed enough of the hostess's cocktails to become impervious to temperature—were dancing in fine spirit, while many of those who could not or would not dance had spilled out into the garden in search of relief and refreshment, and were continuing the festivities there.

Among the earliest guests to arrive were Sir Stanley and Lady Westray, in company with Sir Stanley's daughter from an earlier marriage, Alida, and their charge, Lady Gertrude McAloon, who was looking deceptively feminine and demure in pale pink chiffon. Sir Stanley, for whom any social occasion was a waste of time unless he could talk 'shop' with other men of his type, soon detached himself from the company and was absorbed easily into a group of similar-looking middle-aged and elderly gentlemen who had congregated at the side of the room. Meanwhile, Lady Westray, Alida and Gertie stood and surveyed the room, mentally cataloguing the guests into groups of Unknown, Slight Acquaintances, Allies, Deadly Enemies and Frightful Bores. In between times Gertie was darting the occasional fearful glance over her shoulder. Lady Westray noticed this.

'I don't think Doug's here yet, darling,' she said. 'There's no need to be nervous.'

'I'm not nervous,' lied Gertie.

'I am glad you decided to end it before word got out,' said Lady Westray. 'You would never have suited.'

'I know. It was rather silly of us. He's not too upset, is he?'

'He's been a bit grumpy this week,' began Alida, but her step-mother shot her a warning look.

'He's quite all right,' she said firmly.

A waiter came and furnished them with drinks, and after a mouthful or two Gertie began to feel better. She shook herself. It was most unlike her to think too deeply about the feelings of others, and she had no idea why she was worried about Douglas Westray, who could not *really* have been in love with her given that Tatty had ended things with him only a few weeks ago. Freddy was right: he was much more likely to moon around Tatty than herself. Or perhaps he would not turn up at all. That would be the most sensible thing, from his point of view, and the most gentlemanly way of conducting himself. After all, this party was being attended by not one but *two* of his former fiancées, one of whom would be showing off the new intended for whom she had cast him aside, so where was the sense in his coming? There could not possibly be any fun in it for him.

Just as this thought passed through her head, Tatty Nugent herself made her entrance by the side of her mother, Lady Browncliffe. Entering the room two steps behind them was a tall, handsome young man whose usual wide smile and cheery demeanour had been replaced by an expression which could more accurately be described as agitated and anxious. This was Tom Chetwynd, who had stepped forward to take the place his best friend Douglas Westray had vacated with what some might have considered unseemly haste. Gertie's expression softened for a moment until she saw the young man, after a moment's thought, offer his arm to Miss Nugent, who accepted it with a gracious smile.

'Smug cat!' muttered Gertie to herself.

'Straighten your face, you look like you're thinking of murder,' said a voice next to her. It was Freddy, who had just arrived.

'Wherever have you been?' said Gertie. 'I was expecting you half an hour ago. I am thinking of murder, of course.'

'Well, you needn't make it quite so bristlingly obvious. If they're found dead at the bottom of a cliff tomorrow everybody will know exactly where to look.'

'People like that never die conveniently. They'll get married and have beautiful children and be stinkingly happy, drat them! Fetch me another drink, won't you?'

'But you haven't finished that one yet.'

'Oh, yes I have,' she said, and drained the glass in one gulp. 'And you'd better get a move on if you want to catch me up.'

'My dear girl, you don't suppose I ever arrive at a party stone-cold sober, do you? I started a good two hours ago.' He helped her to another cocktail and took one for himself. 'You ought to be careful—you know you can't hold your drink.'

'I can hold it just as well as you can. Who was it who got stuck up a lamp-post dressed as Tarzan of the Apes after the last Chelsea Arts Ball and had to be rescued by the police?'

'I was perfectly lucid,' said Freddy with dignity. 'It was an unexpected attack of vertigo, that's all.'

'A likely tale. Anyway, I'm just fortifying myself before I go and congratulate Tatty. I shall smile and simper and gush, and jolly well make sure I get an invitation to the wedding.'

She took another large swallow of her drink and departed purposefully towards the happy couple.

'Hallo, Freddy,' said Lady Westray, who was standing close by. 'I didn't know you were coming.'

'Good Lord!' said Freddy. 'If it isn't Lois Sherbourne. Why, I haven't seen you since—when was it?'

'It must be four years at least, I think. Cap Ferrat, do you remember? And it's Lois Westray now. I married Sir Stanley Westray two years ago.'

She indicated across the room to where Sir Stanley Westray, portly and balding, was standing in conversation with a group of elderly men. Freddy took in the scene with an expert glance, then turned back to Lady Westray. As Lois Sherbourne, wife of the famous actor and theatrical impresario David Sherbourne, she had once been known for her wildly successful parties, at which scandalous doings had frequently been rumoured. She was in her late thirties, still very pretty, with chestnut hair that showed not even a strand of grey, and hazel eyes that held a good deal of humour.

'Good Lord!' he said again.

She smiled mischievously at his evident surprise.

'Yes indeed, I'm tremendously respectable now. One can't go on being an *enfant terrible* forever. Sooner or later the years start to tell on one, and instead of looking terribly daring and fashionable, one merely begins to look pathetic.'

'You could never look pathetic,' said Freddy gallantly.

'Thank you, darling.' She lowered her voice. 'The truth of the matter is, after David died it turned out there wasn't any money, and I didn't much like the idea of living my old age in poverty. Then Stanley came along and rescued me. Call me a beastly gold-digger if you will, but I do like him, really I do. He's rather a darling in a pompous, serious sort of way. He needed a woman to look after him after his wife died, and I decided as soon as I met him that I should be that woman.'

'Didn't his children mind?'

'He didn't ask them, as far as I know—but in any case, I threw all my efforts into charming them into submission, and it's all gone rather well. I like them both very much, and I hope they like me. As a matter of fact, Alida and I get along splendidly.'

'And Douglas?'

'He's a fine boy. Things have been a little difficult lately, but I'm sure everything will turn out all right in the end.'

There was a touch of reserve in her manner as she said it.

'Cut up rough, eh?' said Freddy sympathetically.

'Oh! No, nothing like that. He and I rub along very well. But you know how it is—the old stag and the young stag clashing their antlers together. I don't think it's anything too serious.'

She was gazing around the room as she spoke, and seemed inclined to change the subject. She caught sight of something and grimaced.

'Oh dear,' she said.

Freddy turned and saw Sir Stanley talking to another man, who was much taller than he, with a fine head of grey, curly hair and a loud, jovial air about him. As they watched, he burst out laughing, and the sound drifted across the room towards them. This was Lord Browncliffe, Tatty Nugent's father.

'Of course, you know that Walter and Stanley are deadly rivals,' said Lois. 'When Doug and Tatty were engaged they had to reach a sort of truce, but now that's all off they can be as frosty to one another as they like.'

'Lord Browncliffe doesn't look very frosty,' observed Freddy.

'No, and it drives Stanley wild! Walter's one of those terribly loud, hearty people who can't take a hint. Stanley would love to be dignified and distant, but Walter simply won't let him. He likes nothing better than to goad Stanley into a pompous, dignified rage so he can stand and laugh at him. Poor Stanley doesn't have a sense of humour, and falls for it every time. It's awfully naughty of Walter. I suppose I'd better go and intervene, before Stanley gets worked up into a fit of apoplexy.'

She glided off, and Freddy helped himself to another drink from a passing tray.

'Thanks,' said Gertie, coming up just then and taking it neatly from his hand. 'I need another one after that.'

'Bad, eh? Yes, thanks, I will have another. I must say, they don't scrimp on the drinks here. How was Tatty? Did she accept your congratulations graciously?'

'Oh, naturally. One couldn't expect anything less of her.' She downed the drink. 'At any rate, I've done my duty, and it doesn't look as though Doug is going to turn up, so now I can have some fun. Come and dance.'

They danced. The orchestra was very good, the surroundings were attractive, the drinks were strong and plentiful, and Freddy settled in to enjoy himself after a hard day at work. They stopped for another cocktail, then danced again.

'This is rather dull. I think we ought to liven things up a bit,' announced Gertie, as they stumbled a little unsteadily around the floor.

'What do you mean?'

'Well, now that Doug isn't on the scene any more, I'm temporarily unencumbered,' said Gertie. 'As are you, I believe. I propose a contest to see who can collect the most scalps this evening. Hearts may be broken, but never our own. And no great aunts—kisses on the cheek don't count. The loser to pay the winner fifty pounds.'

'I don't have fifty pounds.'

'Nor do I, for that matter. All right then, you shall shout me dinner, just for the look of the thing.'

'Full of yourself, aren't you?' said Freddy. 'That's assuming you win.'

'Of course I'm going to win.'

Freddy cast an assessing glance around the room at likely possibilities. There were plenty of pretty girls of his acquaintance within easy approaching distance, several of whom he knew could generally be relied upon not to snub him. He thought he stood a fair chance.

'We haven't done this in a while,' he said. 'Don't you think we're getting a little old for it?'

'You might be,' said Gertie with dignity. 'I shall be young forever. I expect I'll still be doing this when I'm fifty.'

'I expect you will, and God help us all.'

'Go on, it'll be fun. But we'll have to handicap it. You'd better give me a two-point head start.'

'Whatever for?'

'Why, it's easier for you, as long as you don't mind a slap in the face, because you can just swoop in. I have to be more subtle about it, and wait to be swooped in on.'

'I never swoop in without permission, and I most certainly do mind a slap in the face. In fact, I think you ought to give *me* the head start, because nobody's going to wallop you, are they?'

Gertie waved a hand expressively, and the handicap was eventually conceded to her advantage.

'Good,' she said. 'As for scoring, we'll say one point for a single person, two for married, and an outright win for whoever gets either Tom or Tatty.'

'I'm not kissing Tom.'

'Silly, I'd be awfully jealous if you did.'

'Why, darling, I didn't know you cared so very much about me.'

'I don't care about you at all, ass—oh, bother!'

She turned away suddenly from the door as she spoke.

'What is it?'

'Douglas,' she muttered.

Freddy looked up and saw a young man pushing towards them through the crowd of dancers. He was darkly handsome and slightly dishevelled, with hair that was a little too long.

He stopped next to them, forcing them to stop dancing and shuffle to the side of the floor.

'Hallo, Gertie,' he said. His mouth turned down at the corners, as did his eyes, which gave him something of the look of a tragic basset hound.

'Doug!' exclaimed Gertie brightly. 'I didn't know you were coming. Have you met Freddy?'

The two young men shook hands. As far as Freddy could judge, Douglas Westray must have spent the earlier part of the evening absorbing alcohol into his system with great dedication. He was swaying on his feet a little, and he had evidently decided to save valuable seconds when speaking by eliminating the gaps between his words.

'Listen, Gertie,' he said. 'I've something to say to you. No, really, it's important. You needn't worry, I'm not angry or anything like that—in fact, I've come to the conclusion that this is all for the best, but I can't say what I have to say with this fellow breathing down our necks. Sorry, old chap,' he said to Freddy. 'Now, do come and talk. I'm having the devil of an evening what with one thing and another, but I won't chew your ear off, I promise. I'd just like to have a sensible conversation for once.'

'Oh, very well, then,' said Gertie resignedly. She glanced at Freddy and gave the merest shrug of her shoulders, then allowed herself to be led out of the ballroom. Freddy was left at a loose end, but not for long. A delicate-looking girl nearby gestured to a waiter who was passing with a tray of drinks, but he did not see her. Freddy stopped the waiter and obliged her.

'You're Gertie's friend Freddy, I think,' she said, after she had thanked him. 'I'm Alida. Alida Westray.'

'Ah, of course,' said Freddy. 'Splendid do, what?'

Alida Westray agreed that it was indeed a splendid do, and from there it was most natural for Freddy to ask her to dance. Any hopes he might have had of stealing a march on Gertie were dashed quickly, however, by her manner, which was friendly but distant. He soon discovered why, when Alida smiled at someone over his shoulder and blushed slightly. Freddy turned round and saw a young man standing alone at the side of the ballroom and looking a little awkward.

'Why, if it isn't old Penbrigg!' he said. 'What's he doing here?'

'Leslie? He works for Father. Do you know him?'

'I should say so. He was in the year below me at school, and quite the mechanic. He was always tinkering with things, and building machines that fell apart or exploded unexpectedly. One soon learned never to lend him a watch, as he'd take the thing apart to examine the workings, and when one got it back the minute hand would run backwards and the hour hand would jump forward two hours at a time. So he works for Westray, does he?'

'Yes. He's a terribly clever inventor. I know he's only young, but he's already come up with lots of tremendously useful ideas. He designed a new type of aeroplane wing that very nearly won the Woodville Prize last year.'

'Nearly?'

Her face clouded.

'Well, it ought to have won. But there was a little trouble over the patent. My brother forgot to register it, you see, and then it turned out that Nugent Corporation had been developing the same idea, and they registered their own patent before Westray did and won the competition.'

'I say, bad luck!'

'It was very unfortunate. Leslie took it very well, but I know it must have been galling for him to see the prize go to Nugent Corporation when he'd spent so much time on the idea himself.'

'Rather a coincidence that Nugent just happened to have been developing the same idea at the same time, what?'

'Yes, it is, isn't it?' she said dryly.

Freddy scented a story, but she did not seem inclined to say anything further on the matter at present, so he filed the information away for a future time.

The song had now come to an end, and Freddy led Alida from the floor, where she was immediately claimed by a friend and carried off. Freddy went across to speak to Leslie Penbrigg.

'Hallo, old bean!' he said. 'Where have you been hiding the last few years?'

If any man could have been said to look like an inventor, Leslie Penbrigg was that man. He wore wire-rimmed spectacles that were a little bent at one side, while his hair was untidy and his shirt cuffs peeped out from the sleeves of his dinner-jacket. He had a pleasant face and the air of one whose mind is often elsewhere.

'Freddy!' he said. 'I thought it was you dancing with Alida.'

'It was. She was telling me you work for her father.'

'Yes, I'm very fortunate to have this job. I should never have been happy working for an insurance firm, or the civil service, or something like that, and at Westray Enterprises I'm allowed to tinker with things as much as I like. I've always had a mechanical turn of mind, you know.'

'Yes, I remember. Did you ever get that engine of yours to run on potato peelings?'

'No—I had more luck with cabbage leaves, but I could never get it to run reliably. I abandoned it in the end, but I may go back to it one day.'

'And now you build aeroplanes?'

'Rather. It's a very exciting time for the aircraft industry, with lots of new developments in the offing. Now we can get across the Atlantic there's no saying what will be next. The North Pole, perhaps, if we can build a plane that will withstand the cold.'

He went on in this vein for some time. Freddy noticed he was looking across at Alida as he talked.

'She seems a nice girl,' he said.

'Ah—er—yes,' said Penbrigg, flushing.

'Why don't you ask her to dance?'

'Ah—well, that is—'

'Haven't the nerve, eh?'

'No,' admitted Penbrigg.

'There's no sense in being shy in a place like this. If the fact of her being a girl puts you off then perhaps it might help if you tried to picture her as a sort of internal combustion engine.'

He was joking, but Penbrigg appeared to take it seriously. He regarded Alida Westray, considering.

'Not really,' he said sadly at last. 'Engines are square and grey and ugly and one doesn't have to make witty conversation with them. She's round and pink and pretty, and I dare say won't even look at a fellow who can't be clever. I should only be tongue-tied and she'd think I was an idiot.'

'Far from it. If you can't think of anything to say just talk about the music, or the people you've met, or the old tramp you saw earlier today leading an alpaca down Piccadilly—it doesn't much matter what. If she likes you she won't care what you talk about, and if she doesn't then all the wit in the world won't help you.'

'Oh,' said Penbrigg, as though this were a new idea to him.

Freddy was all for spreading a little happiness, and was about to expand upon his theme when Gertie arrived, slightly flustered and inclined to giggle, and dragged him away.

'One point,' she said smugly.

'I thought you gave him the boot!' said Freddy accusingly.

'Yes, but well, I mean to say, he was practically a sitting duck, so you can't expect me not to take advantage. Call it a goodbye kiss.'

'Hmm. I see I shall have to raise my game.'

Gertie clutched his arm.

'Who's that?' she said excitedly.

Freddy followed her gaze, and saw she was looking at a man who had just arrived. He was perhaps forty, but had the clear advantage over many a younger man as far as appearance was concerned, being handsome with a firm jaw, dashing moustache and a sleek head of hair that was almost certainly his own. Gertie was not the only person to have noticed his arrival; indeed, the eyes of every female guest, young and old alike, seemed to have been turned towards him as though hypnotized. He did not seem to have noticed—or, rather, if he did, the attention did not bother him unduly. He was at present talking to Lady Browncliffe and thanking her for the invitation, while, from her manner, it appeared that she was only too grateful that he had been kind enough to grace her dance with his presence.

'Who is he?' repeated Gertie.

'Don't you recognize him?' said Freddy. 'That's Captain Frank Dauncey, the flying ace. I met him a year or two ago. Retired now, of course, but I think he brought down something like fifty German planes in the war. They gave him so many medals that he must have jangled as he walked. It's a wonder his plane got off the ground, the amount of metal he was wearing at one point.'

'Is that so?' She regarded Captain Dauncey with great interest.

'Isn't he a little old for you?'

'I've always liked older men. They're so tremendously *distinguished.*'

'Well, if you can beat off the throng of swooning women and get anywhere near him, you'll be lucky.'

'Nonsense,' said Gertie, then her face fell as Captain Dauncey was approached by Lord Browncliffe, who shook his hand heartily and bore him away to the safety of a crowd of men. 'Rats!'

'If you can dig him out of that group, then you're cleverer than I thought,' said Freddy.

Just then, a bell rang and supper was announced. Gertie brightened.

'The game's not over yet,' she said, 'but I must say I'm rather hungry.'

'Rather,' agreed Freddy, and they went together into supper.

CHAPTER THREE

WITH GREAT INTREPIDITY, Lady Browncliffe had placed her trust in the British weather, and had decided that supper should be held outside. When Freddy and Gertie emerged from the house, they found that thousands of fairy lights had been strung around the place, giving the garden, which was mostly laid to pavement, an eerie glow against the gathering twilight. The supper was of the buffet sort, and a long table had been placed outside for the purpose, at which a queue had already formed. Behind the table stood several waiters, ready to serve the guests with whatever food they desired, while a stern-looking chef presided behind large joints of meat at one end, brandishing a dangerously sharp carving knife. Besides cold lamb and beef, there was ham, ox tongue, quails, cold salmon and a partridge pie, as well as cakes, wafers, fruit and ices. Freddy and Gertie found themselves a little table at which to perch.

'It's awfully close, still,' remarked Gertie. 'There's no breeze even in this garden.'

'It might be cooler up there,' said Freddy, nodding towards an iron staircase at the side of the house, which led up to an iron balcony that ran along the first floor of the building and acted as a fire escape. Several of the guests had evidently had the same idea of seeking fresh air on higher ground, and were standing on the balcony, looking down upon the assembled guests in the garden below.

'Hallo, there's Douglas again,' said Freddy.

Douglas Westray had just emerged through the French windows into the garden. He stood and swayed a little, then made for their table and collapsed heavily into a chair. He glanced vaguely at the two of them.

'Hallo, Gertie,' he said. 'I didn't know you were coming tonight. Are there any drinks to be had?'

'I should rather have thought you were in need of food, old chap,' said Freddy, who was trying not to laugh at Gertie's outraged expression.

'Perhaps you're right,' he said indistinctly. He made an unsuccessful effort to rise from his seat. 'Lord, I'm fagged all of a sudden! Gertie, be a dear and get me something to eat, would you?'

'Freddy will get you some food,' said Gertie sweetly. 'He was just going for me, weren't you, Freddy?'

'Oh, very well,' said Freddy, who had just spied the last piece of a delicious-looking cake, which he had no intention of offering to Gertie. The little party was duly furnished with victuals, and Douglas Westray set upon the food as though he had not eaten for a week. After he had replenished his interior parts to his satisfaction, he threw down his napkin and sat back.

'I oughtn't to have come this evening, I suppose,' he said mournfully.

'Here it comes,' thought Freddy, who recognized the onset of the maudlin stage of intoxication when he saw it. 'Why not?' he said.

'Because nobody wanted me. Gertie thinks I'm a frightful bore—yes you do,' he said, to a noise of protest from Gertie. 'Tatty can't bear the sight of me, and I make Tom feel uncomfortable because he took her off me.'

'He didn't take her off you—she ended it first,' Gertie pointed out.

'It all comes down to the same thing. It's a poor show when one can't trust one's oldest friend to leave one's girl alone. I was all set to forgive him, but after this evening he's ruined it all. As for the Nugents, they were never too keen on my marrying her in the first place, and they'd rather I hadn't come because they're terrified she's going to change her mind about Tom and take me back. But why should she do that? As far as they're concerned Tom Chetwynd has everything—looks, money, political connections, the whole caboodle. His father's Chief of the Air Staff, you know. After the wedding Lord Browncliffe will have the ear of the Government, and will be in the running for all sorts of contracts. I was only ever going to be second best after that. After all, what have I got? I've no money, I'm nowhere near as tall as Tom, and as to connections—why, even my own father is hardly speaking to me. I'm an honourable man—unlike Tom—but nobody cares about that sort of thing these days.'

'Why isn't your father speaking to you?' said Freddy.

'I'm a disappointment to him,' said Douglas dolefully. 'I lost Tatty, which meant Father lost a lot of possible business, since there was no need for Nugent Corporation to work with Westray any more. Then there was something I didn't do but ought to have, and something else he thinks I did but didn't, and altogether he considers me pretty much a dead loss.'

'Is this something to do with a patent, by any chance?' said Freddy, remembering what Alida Westray had said.

'So you've heard about it too, have you? Everybody seems to know about it. Everybody seems to know what a failure I am.'

'What did you do to make him think you're a failure?' said Gertie, who was not a young lady of great tact or finesse.

'I didn't do anything—that's the whole point. I was supposed to register the patent for a new type of aeroplane wing with slots. It was part of an international competition to see who could come up with an invention that would improve stability at low speeds. The slot idea wasn't new, of course, but we'd come up with an entirely new design for it, which was much more effective than earlier types.'

'Ah, yes,' said Freddy. 'The chap who invented it is an old school pal of mine.'

'The chap who invented it?' Douglas Westray's brow lowered and his chin went up, and just for a moment he looked more like a bulldog than a basset hound. 'Hmph. At any rate, it was a Westray Enterprises invention, and we ought to have won the competition.'

'Why didn't you?' asked Gertie.

'Damned if I didn't forget to register the patent,' said Douglas, with the resigned air of one who has made the same confession several times before. 'I was rushing to get away and catch the boat train that day, and there was a problem with the tickets—all rather complicated—but in the confusion the patent forms completely slipped my mind. I got back from Deauville two weeks later, thinking I'd do it then, only to find that Nugent Corporation had pipped us to it. Well, after that there was no chance of our winning the competition. Nugent entered their aeroplane with our wing slot and won the Woodville prize, and we looked like awful idiots.'

'How did they just happen to have the same idea?' said Freddy. 'Seems rather odd.'

Douglas snorted.

'They said they'd been developing the same sort of wing for at least two years before we started, and that it must have been a coincidence, but that was all rot. The similarities were far too great. It was our idea, all right—no doubt about it.'

'But how did they get hold of it?' said Gertie.

'That's just it, don't you see? Father thinks I passed it on to them. I was still engaged to Tatty at the time, and Father thinks I must have let it slip. In the ordinary way of things it wouldn't have mattered very much. If Tatty and I—well, if things had continued, there would probably have been some kind of agreement between the two companies, perhaps even a merger. But it all ended, so there's no chance of an agreement now. Father and Lord Browncliffe can't stand each other.'

'*Was* it you who gave away the secret?' Gertie inquired.

'No!' said Douglas vehemently. 'Of course it wasn't! What do you take me for? I might forget things occasionally, but I'd never pass on trade secrets. I hope I know *that* much. No, it wasn't me, but nothing will convince him, and I've been in his bad books ever since. It's jolly unfair when one's trying to act honourably and help someone else. If he only knew—'

He stopped, and his brows drew down over his eyes again. Whatever he had been about to say was lost, however, because just then there was a call to attention and the crowd gradually fell silent.

'Oh, Lord,' said Douglas. 'Browncliffe's going to make a speech. I don't think I can stand it.'

A pleased-looking Lord Browncliffe had ascended the first few steps of the fire escape so as to be seen by all, and was beckoning to his daughter and her intended to come and be shown off to the assembled guests.

'Delighted you could all come,' he announced in his hearty voice. 'As you know, my wife and I have good reason to celebrate this evening. It isn't news to most of you, but for those of you who have not heard, my daughter has recently announced her engagement to this fine young man, Thomas Chetwynd.' He paused for applause, then went on. 'The name of Chetwynd will undoubtedly be familiar to you—'

Here he wandered off into a digression about Tom Chetwynd's parents, who were abroad and thus unfortunately not able to be present this evening, and then began enumerating the virtues of his daughter and her fiancé. Everyone listened politely, while Tatty, serene, complacent and beautiful in her conquest, glowed under the public gaze.

Douglas had been shifting uncomfortably during the speech, and as it finally drew to a close, before further applause could break out, he stood up and stumbled towards the stairs.

'Good heavens, he's going to make an ass of himself,' murmured Freddy, feeling in his pocket for his notebook. This promised to be interesting. Douglas reached the stairs and shoved past Tom Chetwynd to join Lord Browncliffe where he stood. Tatty looked taken aback.

'Marvellous speech, sir,' bellowed Douglas, clapping. 'Marvellous. Just like to say a few words, if I may.'

'Douglas!' said Sir Stanley, who was standing nearby.

'No—no,' said Douglas, waving a finger admonishingly. 'Never let it be said a Westray was a bad sport.' He turned and shook hands with a reluctant Lord Browncliffe, then did the same to Tom Chetwynd. 'Tatty, congratulations. I can see you've made your decision. I was always a poor sort of chap, the sort who comes in second or third in the race. I suppose I was never going to get a look-in when Tom came along. I wish you all the best.'

This last was said in a tone of great sincerity, and there were one or two silent sighs of relief as the watchers came to the conclusion that while young Douglas was evidently very drunk, he had not wholly lost control of his faculties, and that total embarrassment was likely to be narrowly avoided. Alas, they reached this conclusion too soon, because Douglas immediately afterwards ruined it all. He had started to turn away as though finished, but at the last minute he turned back suddenly, fixed Tom Chetwynd with a contemptuous glare, and said loudly:

'Let's not worry that he's an unprincipled bounder of the worst sort, and not to be trusted around any decent woman, shall we? For shame, Tom! For shame!'

There was a collective intake of breath, and a few of the guests shuffled uncomfortably. Tom Chetwynd looked pale and shocked. He swallowed.

'Now, look here—' he began. He stepped forward, his hands raised placatingly, but Douglas mistook the gesture. He put up his fists and began to dance on his toes.

'So it's like that, is it? You think that's the way to settle this?'

'No!' said Tom, and retreated hurriedly. But Douglas had begun to work himself up into a temper.

'Come on, then,' he said. 'Let's see if you're really the man you're made out to be!'

He took a swing at Tom, missed, staggered, and almost fell over. There were more gasps, and one or two screams. Freddy glanced at Gertie and saw that she was watching the scene with malicious enjoyment.

'Douglas, stop it!' exclaimed Tatty.

Douglas turned to her, and his expression softened. He took her hands.

'Tatty, don't marry this blighter. I'm the better man, even if I am a little shorter.'

'Douglas!' snapped Sir Stanley, who was now moving through the crowd towards his son.

'What do you want?' said Douglas rudely. 'Can't a man speak to his girl without being interrupted?'

Tatty felt it was time to act, for it looked as though Tom Chetwynd, Lord Browncliffe and Sir Stanley were on the point of laying hands on Douglas and were prepared to do him bodily injury.

'Come inside and we can talk,' she said gently. 'Here in front of everybody is hardly the place for it. Let's go and find a quiet room somewhere. That's right, come in now, and let everyone finish their supper.'

She led him off, and left the guests wondering whether they were supposed to applaud or not. Lord Browncliffe and Tom Chetwynd conversed for a few moments in low voices, then followed Tatty and Douglas indoors.

'What a swizz!' said Gertie in disappointment. 'I was hoping for a black eye or two, at least.'

'Yes, nothing worth printing there,' said Freddy, and put his notebook back in his pocket. 'I'll show it to old Bickerstaffe, but I dare say he won't be interested in anything less than a wholesale brawl.'

'Oh, well, you'd better get me another drink, then. Now that supper's out of the way everyone will be dancing, and you may remember we agreed to a contest.'

'So we did, and may the best man win.'

'Or woman,' said Gertie. 'I'm going to look for Captain Dauncey.'

'You'd be better off going for the easy pickings.'

'We'll see,' she said, then took her drink and departed.

Chapter Four

ALTHOUGH HE HAD readily accepted the gauntlet thrown down before him, Freddy found that his heart was not really in it, for there were too many other things to think about, and his mind was busy. After the contretemps in the garden he could not shake off the feeling that something was very wrong. There was nothing he could quite put his finger on, but his reporter's nose was twitching and telling him that something momentous had happened or was going to happen. Whether it were something to do with what had happened between Douglas Westray and Tom Chetwynd he could not say, but he was determined to keep half an eye out, at least. So it was that, while he danced with several girls who would almost certainly have been quite amenable to his advances had he been disposed to make them, his mind was elsewhere, and after an hour his points tally was still at nought. Gertie had disappeared—he did not know where; presumably in pursuit of Captain Dauncey—but he supposed she would soon turn up and crow at him for his lack of success. He went outside, where many people had remained after supper. It was dark now, but an array of bright lights had been switched on, making it seem almost like day. The air was still uncomfortably close, and he sat down at an empty table to smoke a cigarette.

'Hallo, Freddy,' said Lois Westray. He looked up and saw her emerging from the darkness down the iron staircase from the fire escape.

'Where's Douglas?' he said.

She grimaced.

'Gone home to sleep it off, I hope. Poor Stanley, he's terribly cross.'

'I'm not surprised.'

'I do wish he'd stayed sober. He promised faithfully he wouldn't cause any trouble. Of course, he wasn't any too pleased about Tom and Tatty's engagement, but Tatty had made it clear things were finished between them so he could hardly stand in their way. As a matter of fact, I thought he'd more or less reconciled himself to it—he said as much this morning—but it seems he changed his mind.' She sighed. 'There'll be a row tomorrow, if I'm not much mistaken.'

She went off, and Freddy continued to smoke in silence. After a minute or so he heard footsteps and glanced up to see Captain Dauncey coming down the stairs too. There was no sign of Gertie. Perhaps she had decided to take the most sensible approach and aim for the easier targets. He went back inside, and to his surprise saw Tatty Nugent sitting alone in a corner, concentrating very hard on a glass of champagne. From her manner, he suspected that it was not her first.

'Hallo, Freddy,' she said as he approached. 'I'm having a beastly evening.'

'I expect you are,' he said sympathetically. 'Has Douglas gone home?'

'I hope so. I've had the most awful row with Tom about him. I did love him, you know.'

'Tom or Douglas?'

'Who do you think? But he was impossible. And now Tom's being impossible too, so I'm going to sit here and drink until it all goes away.'

'That's the spirit!' said Freddy.

She finished the last mouthful of champagne and stood up a trifle unsteadily.

'Men are stupid,' she announced with a hiccup. 'Tom is stupid and Douglas is stupid. I don't want either of them any more. Ask me to dance, Freddy.'

Freddy knew better than to argue with a woman in this mood, and besides, there was a reckless air about her which he recognized, and which caused a wicked little idea to dart into his head. It was not one of his nobler schemes, but everybody else seemed to be behaving badly and he did not wish to be left out. Besides, it was perfectly obvious that she had the same idea, since she ignored the dance floor entirely and dragged him out of the room and behind a large potted palm tree in the vestibule. Their tête-à-tête concluded to the satisfaction of both—given that one of them had a point to prove and the other a bet to win—then Tatty observed that people were starting to leave so she had better go and do her duty. She swayed off, and Freddy wandered back into the ballroom in no little state of complacency, then fell into conversation with Lord Browncliffe and Leslie Penbrigg. It was now approaching midnight, and the guests were drifting away. Freddy saw Lois Westray and Alida preparing to leave in company with Gertie, who was looking rather the worse for wear. She tottered across to him and slapped him playfully on the arm with an evening-glove.

'Where did you disappear to?' she said. 'I've been having all sorts of fun.'

'So I see,' said Freddy. 'Look at the state of you—I told you you couldn't hold your drink.'

'Nonsense, I'm completely sober,' said Gertie, who was never one to let mere facts get in the way of a bold assertion.

'Yes you are, and I've no doubt you'll be up early tomorrow morning for a bracing walk in the country followed by a long session of prayer and contemplation.'

'What? No fear of that! Anyway, I was a tremendous success. At least, I think I was. Weren't we supposed to be competing for points, or something? I can't remember. Or if we were, I lost count about an hour ago.'

'We were, and it sounds as though you did a lot better than I did. It's been a dry evening, all told.'

'Splendid! Then I win.'

'Not at all,' said Freddy serenely.

'What do you mean?'

'I *seem* to recall there was a clause in the contest rules that allowed for an outright victory.' He glanced around and whispered in her ear. Her eyes widened.

'*Tatty*? You didn't!' she exclaimed. 'How on earth did you manage that?'

'All thanks to my natural charm,' said Freddy.

'Rot!'

'Well, if you must know, it was hardly a conquest. She'd just had a row with Tom and Douglas, and was in the frame of mind to tell everybody to go hang. She might have picked anybody, really, but it just so happens that I was there at the time so she latched on to me.'

'Bother!' said Gertie. 'If I'd known you were going to be ungentlemanly about it, I'd never have added that clause. In fact, if you were any sort of gentleman at all you'd never have agreed to the contest in the first place, so I think I deserve extra points for that.'

'You can have as many points as you like but I still win on trumps,' said Freddy.

She glared at him, but Lady Westray was beckoning, for they were about to leave.

'Hmph! Very well, we shall continue this discussion another time,' she said. She stifled a yawn. 'But be warned, I may demand a recount.'

She went off, and Freddy began to think about leaving too.

'Are you joining us, Freddy?' said Lord Browncliffe. 'A few hands of cards, by way of cooling down in a nice quiet way, away from the women and all the noise.'

'Why not?' said Freddy.

'Jolly good. Dauncey's joining us, and Tom. What about you, Penbrigg? It'll be a relief to sit down after all these hours standing,' said Browncliffe.

'It certainly will,' said Penbrigg fervently. 'Yes, I suppose I might stay a little while, thank you, sir.'

'We'll go into the library,' said Browncliffe. 'We can leave my wife and Tatty to deal with the clearing up. That's women's stuff.'

He led them into a comfortable library which also acted as his study. He called it a library, but there were few books in evidence: just the usual collection of dictionaries, encyclopaedias and atlases, as well as a whole shelf full of stories about big-game hunting and other similar adventures in which humans did battle against various representatives of the lower orders of the animal kingdom and the animals came off worst. Freddy remembered that Lord Browncliffe's hunting exploits had often appeared in the newspapers, and he had made quite a name for himself as a marksman.

'Whisky? Or will you have a brandy?' said Browncliffe. 'No, it's all right, Whitcomb, you may go and help the ladies with the clearing up. We'll manage for ourselves. Now, what shall it be: Nap, Banker or Pontoon?'

The butler departed, drinks were poured and cigars were lit, and the men settled down to important business.

'You're fond of shooting, I take it, sir,' said Freddy, as cards were dealt and money pledged. He was looking at a large glass case which held a selection of guns ranging from tiny pistols to enormous shotguns.

'I most certainly am,' said Lord Browncliffe. 'Do you shoot much?' Without waiting for Freddy to reply, he embarked upon a long anecdote about a tiger hunt in India, in which his quarry had cunningly eluded him for three days, only to be bested at last thanks to Lord Browncliffe's tenacity, his ability, and his Westley Richards Patent Double .425 bore Nitro Express rifle (a snip at eighty-two guineas). 'Had the head mounted, of course,' he said. 'It's not here though—we keep it down at our place in the country. I have a much bigger collection of guns there, too. This is just a selection for show.'

He leaned back in his chair, turned a key and pulled open the glass door of the case, for the better viewing of its contents, then frowned.

'That's odd. Where's the Colt revolver? I'm sure it was here the other day. Or did I take it down to Sussex? I suppose I must have.'

'Don't you keep the guns locked up?' said Freddy.

Lord Browncliffe waved a hand.

'I know, I know. Remiss of me, really. Lady Browncliffe is always telling me I ought to, but I'm afraid I forget. I'm in and out of the case so often, you see.'

He seemed to forget about the missing gun, and began to relate another exploit.

'Tom shoots too, don't you?' he said at last. 'Didn't you say you once killed a grizzly bear out in the Rocky Mountains?'

'That's right,' said Tom colourlessly.

'Well, come on, boy, out with the story!'

'There's nothing much to tell. It turned up and I shot it, that's all.'

Browncliffe tried again, but Tom was unwilling or unable to join in the spirit of the evening, so Browncliffe gave it up and returned his attention to the game. Freddy regarded Tom Chetwynd covertly. He seemed subdued and preoccupied, although from what Freddy had been told this was most unlike his usual self. Perhaps he was upset at having been attacked by the man who had once been his best friend.

So the evening wore on. The men became quieter and the room smokier as the game progressed. Freddy was amused to see that Lord Browncliffe was not an especially good loser. He humphed and harrumphed whenever he lost a hand, but was forced to pretend not to mind. Captain Dauncey played with some success, while Tom Chetwynd seemed to have cast all caution to the winds, and was gambling his money recklessly with a sort of grim determination. Freddy made a few modest wins, but then began to lose money to Leslie Penbrigg, who was doing much better than any of them. At last, Freddy threw in his cards and said:

'You've cleaned me out, old chap. You're far too good at this game. If it wouldn't lead to your challenging me to a duel, I'd almost say you weren't playing fair.'

'Oh, well,' said Penbrigg, almost apologetically. 'I find it helps if one keeps a clear head.'

Freddy noticed that he had not touched his drink.

'Ha, so that's the secret, is it?' he said.

'Bad luck for me that you're sober, my boy,' said Lord Browncliffe jocularly. 'I won't be able to pump you about what's going on at Westray. It was just your bad luck we got there first with the new wing slot design, but I'm sure you've got plenty of other ideas up your sleeve, eh?'

'One or two,' agreed Penbrigg with a smile.

'Very young to have such a high position at Westray, aren't you?' said Captain Dauncey. 'Sir Stanley must think an awful lot of you.'

'I—I hope he does,' said Leslie Penbrigg, who had gone slightly pink. Freddy guessed he was thinking of Alida Westray.

'You worked under old Finkley, didn't you?' said Browncliffe.

'That's right, sir.'

'I heard the old chap went ga-ga. Experience is all very well, but at a certain age the brain starts to disintegrate, and then a man is good for nothing any more.'

'He was jolly kind to me, and taught me a lot,' said Penbrigg. 'I'm awfully grateful to him.'

'I'm going all in,' announced Tom Chetwynd, who, on the contrary, had helped himself generously to Lord Browncliffe's whisky.

'What the devil is that racket?' said Browncliffe, as the sound of some commotion drifted into the library from outside. 'Why can't they keep the noise down when they're clearing up? How's a fellow supposed to concentrate on his game?'

Just then, the door opened and Whitcomb the butler entered.

'I beg your pardon, my lord,' he said, 'but her ladyship has asked me to come and fetch you.'

'Come and fetch me? Why couldn't she come here herself if she wanted something?' said Browncliffe irritably.

'It is a matter of a stuck door, my lord.'

'But why bother me with it? Be off with you and fix it yourself. Shall we have another hand?'

The butler hovered. Lord Browncliffe glanced up at him.

'Well, what is it?'

'It's not a question of fixing the door so much as breaking it down, my lord. It appears that somebody has somehow managed to bolt her ladyship's dressing-room door from the inside.'

Lord Browncliffe regarded his butler with a pained expression.

'I don't know what you're talking about, but I can see I'm going to get no peace until I come. Oh, very well.'

He rose heavily to his feet and followed the butler out of the room, then returned a minute or two later, a puzzled look on his face.

'Dashed odd!' he said. 'He's right—someone's bolted the door from the inside and we can't get it open. I've no idea how it happened.'

'Perhaps one of the guests went in there and fell asleep,' suggested Freddy.

'Yes, well, it's damned inconvenient. I don't want to break the door down, but all Lady Browncliffe's things are in there and she's kicking up an awful fuss about it.'

'Let's go and see,' said Tom.

They all rose and followed Lord Browncliffe up the staircase to the first floor. There they found Lady Browncliffe and a very tired-looking Tatty standing with Whitcomb and a pair of housemaids. They were all staring at the door.

'Are you sure it's bolted and not just stuck?' said Captain Dauncey. He tried the door. 'No, it's bolted right enough.' He bent down and peered through the keyhole. 'The lights are on but I can't see much. Ah, what's that? Someone's fallen asleep in the chair, I think. A man. I can just see his foot.'

Freddy was getting that odd feeling again, as though something were very wrong.

'Let me see,' he said. Captain Dauncey stepped aside obligingly and Freddy applied his eye to the keyhole. After a second he straightened up.

'Is there any other way into this room?' he said.

Something in his tone must have struck them all, for they stared at him in concern.

'No—' began Lady Browncliffe, but Tatty said:

'Only through the window, but I imagine it's fastened.'

She glanced at the butler for confirmation.

'Yes,' he said. 'I was most careful to fasten the upstairs windows before the dance began.'

'Whoever's in there might have opened it again to let some air in,' said Dauncey.

'Let's go and see,' said Freddy. 'But if it's closed we still have to get in one way or another. Does anyone have a knife? Or are there any tools in the house we might use? I don't have anything myself, I'm afraid.'

All the men felt in their pockets. Lord Browncliffe brought out a pack of cigars, some matches, a length of string and some money, while Penbrigg produced a crumpled handkerchief, several assorted nuts and bolts, and a toy whistle. Dauncey had some money and a small penknife, of the sort that is carried on a key-ring. Tom Chetwynd, meanwhile, fumbled in his pockets distractedly and spilled the contents out onto the floor.

'Now that's what I call a penknife,' said Dauncey, and indeed Tom had dropped an implement which seemed to indicate that he had been expecting to spend a week in the wilderness, trapping squirrels and building a shelter from fallen tree-branches, instead of attending a London society ball.

'You dropped this,' said Freddy, handing Tom a letter.

'Ah, yes, thanks,' said Tom, shoving it hurriedly into his inside pocket. 'It's a letter from my mother in Paris—just arrived this morning.'

'Shall I go and look in the tool-box, sir?' said Whitcomb.

'No need just yet,' said Freddy. 'I think Chetwynd's knife might do. The fire escape runs along the outside of the window, I believe. Is that right?'

'Yes,' replied Lady Browncliffe.

'What are you going to do?' asked Tatty.

'I hope I'm going to get in without breaking anything,' said Freddy.

He set off down the stairs, followed by Tom Chetwynd and Captain Dauncey. Once out in the garden, they ran up the iron stairs and along the fire escape, and stopped outside a window. The heavy curtains were drawn, and only a chink of light showed through a gap at the top.

'Closed,' said Freddy. 'Is this the right room?' He glanced along at the other windows outside which the balcony ran. 'Yes, it must be this one.'

He took the penknife and slid the blade in between the two sashes.

'This will only work if the catch is loose,' he said.

'Go in for burglary much, do you?' said Dauncey.

'Only when things are quiet at the paper. Hmm, it's stiff, but I think with a little pressure—' He frowned in concentration. 'Ah! There we have it! Should be able to open it now.' He pushed at the sash, which opened with a loud creak. 'In we go,' he said, then climbed over the window-sill and disappeared behind the curtains.

Dauncey and Tom Chetwynd followed, then both stopped dead. The room was decorated in feminine style, with floral wallpaper and many ornamental touches. In one corner stood a tall looking-glass, near a lady's dressing table surmounted by another, smaller glass. Against one wall stood a writing desk of the folding out sort, while just to the right of the window was a chair. In this chair was Douglas Westray, who was now beyond all hope of ever persuading Tatty to come back to him. He sat, his legs sprawled out in front of him, his eyes wide and staring. Down the right side of his head and over his ear was spread a dark-coloured substance that looked at first glance like oil. His right arm dangled over the arm of the chair, and on the floor below his right hand was a pistol.

'Good God! He's dead!' exclaimed Dauncey.

Freddy gazed at the scene, taking in all the details.

'So now we know where Lord Browncliffe's Colt revolver went,' he said. 'He really ought to have kept that case locked.'

There was something like a choking sound behind him, and he turned to see Tom Chetwynd, who was white in the face and swaying a little.

'Are you all right?' said Freddy. 'He was your friend, wasn't he? I'm sorry.'

Tom said:

'Well, if that doesn't cap it all! Poor old Doug,' and began to laugh hysterically in great gasps.

'Better try and get a hold of yourself, old thing,' said Freddy gently.

Tom took a deep breath and did as suggested.

'Sorry,' he said. 'I'm all right now.'

Dauncey stepped forward.

'Better not touch anything,' said Freddy, and Dauncey brought himself up short.

'I suppose not. What do we do now?'

At that moment, there was a hammering on the door.

'We let events take their course,' said Freddy, and went to unbolt the door.

CHAPTER FIVE

THREE WEEKS LATER, Freddy returned to the offices of the *Clarion* after a morning spent outside to find Gertie waiting for him. She had made herself comfortable, and was at present sitting back in his chair with her feet up on his desk, much to the discomposure of Jolliffe, who was doing his best to keep his eyes away from her trim and well-proportioned legs.

'Beastly drizzle today,' she remarked. 'I'm not sure which is worse—this, or that fearful heat.'

'At least I can think now it's cooler,' said Freddy. 'Anyway, to what do I owe the pleasure of this visit? Have you come to pay me my fifty pounds?'

'Don't be ridiculous—I never promised you fifty pounds. No, as a matter of fact, it's something serious. You were at the inquest on Friday, weren't you?'

'I was. Rather a depressing show all round, what? I mean to say, one doesn't like to think that life could ever become so dire that one felt the need to exit the stage.'

Gertie sat up and lowered her legs, somewhat to Jolliffe's relief.

'Yes, but that's just it—he didn't kill himself. They got it all wrong!'

'What do you mean, they got it all wrong? Of course he killed himself. How could it possibly have been otherwise?'

'I don't know—I just know it wasn't suicide.'

'My dear girl, he bolted himself in and blew his brains out. That's suicide by any definition.' But Gertie was shaking her head vehemently, so he said, 'What do you think happened, then?'

'I've no idea.'

'Then why do you think it wasn't suicide?'

'Because he had no reason for it,' said Gertie.

'Of course he did. He had lots of reasons: Tatty threw him over, then you threw him over—that's two, to start with. He'd disgraced himself with his father through his own incompetence. How many reasons do you need?'

'Oh, there was nothing serious between Douglas and me. I spoke to him on the evening of the dance, remember? He was perfectly happy after I left him. He admitted it had been stupid of him to ask me, and I admitted I'd been stupid to say yes, then we both laughed and made it up, and everything was hunky-dory between us.'

'Yes, I remember,' said Freddy dryly.

'What do you remember? I don't have awfully clear memories of that night. Did I do something silly?'

'No more than usual. But anyway, even if you parted on good terms, he was still pretty glum that whole evening, you have to admit. Why, he even came and sat at our table and explained at length how miserable he was, and how his father was angry with him because of his mistake about the wing slot patent.'

'But didn't you say that happened last year? I expect Westray have patented lots of inventions and won all sorts of prizes since then. Douglas and his father had been at loggerheads for years over one thing or another. It wasn't the sort of thing that would drive him to suicide. Besides, that was how Doug was. He was a dreadful bore when he'd been drinking, but he would have been all right the next day, I know it. Tatty agrees with me—she spoke to him too, and you shall hear her story later. But there was something else. I didn't remember it at the time, because I was rather—er—tired that night—' (here Freddy raised his eyebrows) '—but it came to me a few days later something he said while we were talking. He said he was puzzling over something, and didn't know what to do.'

'Puzzling over what?'

'That's just it. I wish I could remember. He was feeling upset that evening, because he'd found something terrible out and he was in a quandary as to what to do about it.'

'What had he found out?'

'He didn't say—at least, I don't think he did. It was something he'd discovered which was bad enough in itself, but he'd been thinking about it and suddenly realized it was even worse than he thought, and would raise an awful stink if it came out. It was just a suspicion, and he had no proof, and he was wondering whether he ought to act or let it lie.'

Freddy was sceptical.

'I don't suppose it's very important,' he said. 'And even if it is, that still doesn't alter the fact that he was discovered in a room which was locked on the inside, and that his were the only finger-prints on the gun. I take it that *is* what you're suggesting? If he didn't shoot himself, then someone else must have done it. Or do you suspect an accident?'

'Well, I *didn't*, but do you think it might have been?' said Gertie hopefully.

Freddy grimaced.

'I don't see how. The rest of his actions were pretty deliberate. After all, he went into Lord Browncliffe's study, took a gun out of the cabinet, loaded it, then took it all the way upstairs to Lady Browncliffe's dressing-room and locked himself in. Why did he do that, if he wasn't intending to shoot himself? I don't know about you, but I'm not in the habit of playing with revolvers just for the fun of it—especially not at other people's evening-parties. No, whatever happened, it was deliberate all right. So if Westray didn't do it himself, then who did, and how?'

'I don't know, but it must have happened somehow,' said Gertie. 'Listen, I came here because Tatty wants to talk to you too. She doesn't believe Doug killed himself any more than I do, and she wants you to come and have a scout around at the house.'

'Why me? Surely if she suspects something then she'd be better off calling the police.'

'They won't listen. The verdict of the inquest was quite clear—suicide. Even if I tried to talk to them they wouldn't be interested. But you've done a bit of detective-work in the past, haven't you?'

'Oh, well, just a little,' said Freddy modestly.

'Then come with me to St. James's Square and see Tatty. All you have to do is hear what she has to say, and see if you can spot anything the police might have missed.'

Freddy suspected that Gertie's activity in this matter sprang mainly from guilt at the thought that she might have been partly responsible for Douglas Westray's suicide, but did not voice this thought.

'Wherefore this sudden friendship with Tatty?' he said instead. 'I thought she was your deadly rival.'

'We are companions in misery,' said Gertie piously. 'We women ought to stick together in such circumstances. And besides, after what she got up to with you at the party I decided that perhaps she wasn't such a bad old thing after all.'

'Awfully convenient, your memory, isn't it? You remember what Tatty and I got up to, but not what you got up to yourself.'

'What are you talking about? I didn't get up to anything.'

'Q. E. D,' said Freddy dryly.

'But you will come, won't you? Let's go now—she ought to be in.'

'I can't go now, I have work to do,' said Freddy.

'Later, then.'

Freddy sighed. He did not think there was much use in it, but he knew Gertie would never leave him alone unless he agreed to it.

Oh, very well,' he said grudgingly.

'That's more like it. I shall come and fetch you at six o'clock. Make sure you're finished by then.'

She went out, and left Freddy to get on with his work.

Badenoch House looked very different in the early evening drizzle from when Freddy had last seen it, three weeks earlier at the summer ball. The black front door was no longer thrown wide open, and the grand columns that stood to either side of it seemed to be huddling around it as though to protect it from the rain. On applying to the butler, they were informed that Miss Nugent was at home and would see them. They were taken into a comfortable sitting-room on the first floor, whose windows overlooked the garden and the fire escape. Tatty was sitting in an armchair, reading a book. She rose to greet them as they were shown in.

'I've brought Freddy,' announced Gertie unnecessarily. 'He doesn't believe a word of it, but I said you'd convince him.'

Now that Freddy came to look more closely at Tatty, he saw that she looked worn and tired, and that her eyes were rimmed with pink.

'Hallo, Freddy,' she said.

'I say, I'm awfully sorry about Douglas,' he said.

She turned her head away.

'So am I, but as you can imagine I can't exactly wail about it in public. It wouldn't look quite the thing, would it?'

'I suppose not. But do you really think there's any use in raking it all up? It won't bring the poor chap back.'

'No, it won't, but I'd swear he wasn't in the frame of mind to kill himself that evening. I'm sure of it.'

Freddy thought that Tatty, too, was feeling guilty, and wanted to convince herself that she had had nothing to do with Douglas's death. But he had promised to listen to what she had to say, so he said:

'Gertie says you don't think he was unhappy.'

'He was never *happy*, as such. He was the mournful sort as a rule, but don't you see? He enjoyed it. That was the way he was. He got great satisfaction out of looking on the gloomy side of things. It cheered him up in an odd sort of way.'

'Do you mean to say he was happy that you and he had broken off your engagement, and that you were going to marry Chetwynd?' said Freddy.

'No, of course not. He was upset enough about that, I won't deny it. But when he interrupted Father's speech that night, I thought I'd better do something to stop him ruining the party any more than he already had, so we went to be by ourselves and have a little chat.'

She stared at the floor. Freddy might almost have said that she looked slightly sheepish.

'Well?' he said. 'Go on. What did he say that makes you so sure he wasn't unhappy?'

She looked even more uncomfortable.

'It's not so much what he said, as what I said. I'm not proud of it, but I'm rather afraid I may have led him to believe that I might reconsider.'

'Did you indeed? Did you mean it?'

'Yes—no—I don't know! I was terribly confused. Doug was worked up and a bit incoherent, and said that Tom wasn't good enough for me, and I could see he was going to start talking and never stop, so I said the first thing I could think of to keep him quiet. I told him I'd been having second thoughts about Tom, but that now wasn't the time to talk about it. I said I should think about it overnight, and that we'd talk about it in the next day or two with clear heads.'

'And what did he say to that?'

'He perked up, and seemed much happier. Of course, I knew he'd been drinking, and I knew that it was more than likely that once he'd sobered up he'd realise what an ass he'd made of himself and would come and beg pardon.'

'Did he really want you back?'

Tatty grimaced.

'I don't know. He said he did, but I thought it was just the drink talking. We used to row all the time, you know, and I thought he must have been as secretly relieved as I was when I broke it off. At any rate, when I sent him away that evening with a promise to think about it I swear he was happy—or happier, at least. He apologized for interrupting Father's speech, and we agreed that we'd talk about it in a day or two, when there was more time.'

'Did you see him after that?' asked Freddy.

She shook her head.

'No. He went off, and I didn't see him again for the rest of the evening. I thought he must have gone home, and I was glad of it, because then Tom came and we had a row about him, and I was glad Doug wasn't there to hear it. I had no idea he'd stayed at the party. It was an awful shock when we found out what had happened. I still can't understand how it *did* happen.

I mean, he seemed all right when he went away—or as all right as he ever was. I'd promised to think about taking him back, so why did he go away and shoot himself? It doesn't make sense.'

'Could something else have happened in the meantime?'

'Such as what?'

'Well, there was this matter of the patent last year.'

'That was all in the past,' she said. 'Sir Stanley was very angry with Doug at the time, it's true, but I don't see why the whole thing should have driven him to kill himself *now*.'

'Perhaps it was one thing after another,' suggested Freddy. 'He lost Westray the prize, then he lost you, then Gertie. Perhaps in the end it was all too much for him.'

'Rot,' said Gertie. 'Don't you remember what I told you? He'd found something out about someone that would cause an awful scandal if it were known. What if the person in question decided to put him out of the way to stop him from revealing the secret?'

'Rather far-fetched, don't you think?'

'No more than the idea that he killed himself.'

They were both glaring at him with a look he recognized well. When two women decided to organize against one man, the result was a foregone conclusion. He sighed.

'Very well, then, assuming for a moment this is all true, and that someone somehow passed through a bolted door by a process of osmosis and killed him, what do you expect me to do about it?'

'Why, help me find out who it was, of course,' said Gertie.

'Help you? Oh, you're going to play detective, are you?'

'Yes, but I can't do it alone. I can question people and that sort of thing, but I'll need you if there's to be any shinning up drainpipes or crawling about in the mud, or for any rough stuff.'

'I'm quite sure you can shin up a drainpipe just as well as I can—which is to say, not at all. And as for rough stuff, I'd much prefer to give it a wide berth if it's all the same to you.'

'Excellent, then that's settled,' said Gertie, who heard only what she wanted to hear, as a rule. 'So, then, where do we start?' She looked at Freddy expectantly.

'I thought you were in charge of this business?'

'Well, yes, I am, but more in the manner of a director of operations. I shall just give you a hint or two if I see you're going wrong.'

'How kind of you. Very well, then, in a case of this sort I should suggest we start with an examination of the scene of the crime—or, should I say, since we don't know for certain it *was* a crime, the scene of the incident.'

'Mother hasn't been too keen on using her dressing-room since it happened,' said Tatty. 'So we can go in whenever you like.'

'Now seems as good a time as any,' said Freddy.

Chapter Six

LADY BROWNCLIFFE'S dressing-room looked much as it had on the night of Douglas Westray's death, although she had removed many of her personal effects from the place. When they entered Gertie went straight across to the window and looked out, while Tatty hovered near the door, a worried frown on her face. Freddy stood in the middle of the room and gazed about him. The place was dim, and there was a faint smell of dust in the air. The heavy blue curtains were open, giving a view out onto the iron balcony and the garden below. Several patterned rugs were laid across the plain carpet underneath. Little tables stood here and there, scattered with ornaments and figurines and photographs in silver frames. On a chest of drawers stood two tall and stately vases, while hung about the walls were portraits and still life paintings done in oils. Lady Browncliffe seemed to be a collector of china, too, for a number of valuable-looking plates were displayed above the picture rails and on the walls to each side of the door. The folding desk was open, and on it were a leather blotter and a pen and ink stand. On one side of the dressing-table stood a sewing-box. The chair in which Douglas Westray had died stood to the right of the window. It was a carved mahogany affair, comfortably upholstered in a floral fabric. Freddy went to examine it. On the top left part of the back cushion there was a rusty streak of something.

'Is that blood?' said Gertie with distaste.

'Looks like it. His head was resting here when we found him. I take it they didn't clean it off?'

'I don't think anybody's been in here since the police finished,' said Tatty.

'Helpful,' said Freddy, looking at the thin film of dust that lay across a nearby table. 'That means if there is any evidence then it ought to be still here.'

He turned his attention to the door. There was nothing special about it. It had a keyhole from which the key was missing, and a bolt about six inches above the door knob.

'Who put this bolt on?' he said.

'It's always been there as far as I know,' said Tatty.

He shut the door experimentally, and shot the bolt, which fastened easily.

'Is there a key?' he said.

'Not that I know of. Not one that we've ever used, anyhow. Most of the doors here don't lock—or if they do I've no idea where the keys are.'

'Does the library door lock?'

Tatty shook her head.

'That's why Doug came up here, of course,' said Gertie. 'He wanted to do it in private.'

'Did he know there was a bolt on this door?' said Freddy, addressing Tatty.

'I dare say he did. He'd been here often enough in the old days,' she replied.

'Hmm,' said Freddy. He rattled the door a little. The bolt stayed fastened. 'Doesn't come loose.'

'No. We tried that night, don't you remember? That's why you had to go in through the window.'

'Yes.'

'I don't know why you're paying so much attention to that door,' said Gertie. 'It's perfectly obvious that the window is the key to it all. Why, anyone might have come along the fire escape and got in that evening. You did yourself.'

'True. But I did it by levering the catch up with a penknife from the outside. If someone did the same thing, then how did they get out and fasten the window again?'

Gertie lifted the catch.

'It's pretty loose,' she said.

She threw open the window, ducked under the sash and vaulted lightly over the window-sill onto the iron balcony, then shut the window again. Freddy and Tatty watched as she rattled the sash and banged the window frame near the catch. After some effort, it fell partly back into place. She motioned at them to let her in again.

'You see? That's how they did it!' she said triumphantly, once she was back in the room. 'The killer came in through the window, killed Doug, then escaped the same way. Or he needn't have come in through the window at all—he might just as easily have arrived through the door and bolted it from the inside before he did the deed.'

'It's a pretty theory,' said Freddy, 'but there are one or two objections. The first is that you made the most awful racket just then. If that's how your imaginary murderer did it, then he would certainly have been noticed banging on the window to fasten it, given that there were dozens of people milling about in the garden and on the balcony at various times. The second is that I'm afraid I loosened that catch myself when I went in that evening. When I tried it, it was quite stiff, and it took me a good few minutes to lever it up. One couldn't possibly have fastened it again merely by giving the window a good whack.'

'Oh, but that must be how it happened,' said Gertie. 'There must be something we've missed, that's all.'

'Perhaps.' Freddy was eyeing the writing-desk. He went across to it and examined it. It had three or four pigeon-holes for correspondence, but all were empty, apart from one, which held a little stack of note-paper printed with Lady Browncliffe's address. The top sheet of the blotter had been used, but only lightly. There were several notes scrawled around the edges, all clearly by Lady Browncliffe herself.

'Why did he come all the way upstairs to kill himself but not write a note?' said Freddy, almost to himself.

'Because he didn't kill himself,' said Gertie. 'That's what we've been trying to tell you.'

Freddy picked up the pen from the stand. It was tortoise-shell with a gold nib.

'He couldn't have written a note anyway—not unless he brought his own pen with him. Look.'

Gertie and Tatty came forward to see. The nib of the pen was bent and twisted and completely ruined.

'I gave that to Mother for her birthday!' exclaimed Tatty in dismay. 'How did it happen?'

'I've no idea,' said Freddy.

'Did she tread on it by accident?' suggested Gertie. 'I've done that with pens before.'

'I don't think so,' said Freddy. 'This has been bent, not squashed. It looks almost as though someone has been trying to lever something up with it.'

'But what?'

Freddy shrugged, then replaced the pen and continued to gaze around the room. He went across to the window and moved the catch up and down to try it for himself. It was less stiff than it had been on the night of Douglas's death.

'I wonder why nobody heard the shot,' he said thoughtfully.

'The band were playing too loudly for anyone to hear anything, as I recall,' said Gertie. 'I was quite deafened.'

'Yes, but still, even then one might have thought somebody in another part of the house—one of the servants, perhaps—would hear it. It's a pity too, because it means nobody knows at exactly what time he died. Didn't the coroner say you were the last person to see him alive, Tatty?'

'Yes, after he interrupted Father's speech and I took him away for our private conversation. Although I'm not sure how private it was, now that I come to think of it,' she added.

'What do you mean?'

'Well, I rather suspected at the time that somebody had overheard us. We were in the smoking-room—that's what we call it, at any rate, but nobody goes in there to smoke, as it's at the front of the house and pretty cold and dark most of the time, so I knew we could be alone there. There's a sort of ante-room leading to it that's used for coats, and while Doug and I were talking I heard the floor outside creak, and I thought someone must have come in for their coat, so I shut the door so as not to be overheard. Then Doug went out and I waited, because it was nice and cool in the smoking-room and I wanted to have a cigarette and think in peace for a few minutes. Whoever it was in the cloak-room had gone by the time I came out, but I wonder whether they mightn't have seen Doug as he passed through. If they did, then they'd have presumably been the last person to see him alive, not me.'

'Any idea who it was?'

'No—that is—' she sighed. 'I was a little frightened at the time that it might have been Tom. He was standing in the hall talking to Father when I came out, and he gave me a terribly frosty look—or at least, I thought he did. Afterwards I told myself I was just feeling guilty about what I'd done, or that perhaps he'd seen Douglas coming out just before me and wasn't happy that we'd been talking alone together. At any rate, he never brought it up, even when we were rowing later, so I can only assume he didn't hear what was said.'

'What time was it?'

'It must have been just after ten, I think.'

'And nobody's known to have seen Douglas after that,' said Freddy. 'We found him at half past one, so that's three and a half hours in which it could have happened—or rather less, I should say, because the band had stopped playing and most people were leaving or had left by midnight, and the house was a lot quieter, so someone would have likely heard the shot if it had happened later than that. Yes, I think we can safely assume it happened during the party. Now, what—?'

He gazed around the room again, trying to cast his mind back to the night of the dance and how the room had looked then, when he had come in through the window and found Douglas's body. Something seemed different, although he could not think what it might be. He frowned, racking his brains, then at last gave it up.

'I don't think there's anything else to see here,' he said. 'It all seems straightforward enough. Shall we leave this room to its memories?'

They went out and downstairs, and found that Lady Browncliffe had just arrived home.

'Mother, what happened to your pen?' said Tatty.

'Why, what do you mean, dear? Which pen?'

'The one I got you for your birthday. You know, the tortoise-shell one. It's broken.'

'Broken?'

'Yes. The nib's all bent and twisted.'

'Are you sure?' said Lady Browncliffe. 'How did that happen?'

'I don't know. We just found it in your dressing-room like that, in its stand.'

'In my dressing-room? Oh, of course. I wondered why I hadn't seen it lately. I must have forgotten to bring it out when we shut the room up. Can it be mended, do you think?'

'It'll need a new nib, at the very least,' said Tatty.

'Oh dear,' said her mother. 'I'm sure the servants have been in that room, gawping. Terribly ghoulish, really, but people will be curious. I dare say somebody broke it while they were looking around. One of them snapped a tooth off my silver comb, too.'

'What's that?' said Freddy.

'I had everything brought out of there after Douglas died, you see. I'm not the sensitive sort, as a rule, but I couldn't quite bear to sit and preen in front of a glass, knowing what had happened there. But someone must have broken the comb when they brought it out—either Sally or Mabel, I suppose, although they both denied it. Anyway, I must have a word with Whitcomb about the damage. It really is too careless of them.'

'Might I see the comb?' said Freddy.

'If you like,' said Lady Browncliffe. 'Tatty, fetch it for me, would you?'

The comb was brought, and Freddy took it and examined it. It was the decorative sort for holding back a lady's hair, in delicate silver with only two prongs—or rather one, since the other had been snapped clean off. Lady Browncliffe regarded it mournfully.

'Your father brought it back from Paris,' she said. 'I was very fond of it. I do wish people would be more careful.'

There seemed nothing else to see, so they took their leave, and Tatty went to show them out.

'By the way,' she hissed to Freddy, as Gertie went on ahead. 'You'd better not get any ideas.'

'About what?' said Freddy in surprise.

'You know. Just because you caught me unawares at the dance, don't think it meant anything. And you'd better not tell anybody.'

'I'm not quite sure what you're referring to,' said Freddy politely. 'I regret to say I'd had a few too many cocktails that evening, and I don't remember much about it. Did I tread on your foot while we were dancing? I'm awfully sorry.'

'Good. Just you make sure you don't do any inconvenient remembering,' she said sharply. Then her manner changed, and she sighed. 'What do you think about Douglas? Am I making something out of nothing? I've wondered and wondered whether it mightn't just be the guilt making me act. One doesn't like to think one might be responsible for someone else's death.'

'My dear girl, you're not responsible for what Douglas did,' he said. 'He was a grown man, and if he wanted to kill himself there's nothing you could have done to stop him.'

'But do you think he did kill himself?'

'I haven't seen anything yet to make me think he didn't,' said Freddy slowly.

'I was afraid you'd say that,' she said, and gave him a sad little smile.

Chapter Seven

Gertie had a theatre engagement, so Freddy saw her into a taxi and she went off, still proclaiming that her theory was correct. Freddy was unconvinced, but he had promised to look into it, and so he went back to his rooms on Fleet Street and read through the notes he had taken at the inquest into Douglas Westray's death. There was not much to look at. Douglas had died at some time between ten o'clock and half past one on the evening of Thursday the 19th of June, and the cause of death was a bullet in his right temple. There were no other injuries to the body. The deceased was found in a room that was bolted from the inside, and was known to have been in a depressed state of mind on the evening in question, so the coroner had had no hesitation in recommending that a verdict of suicide be brought. It seemed clear enough that that was what had happened, and Freddy set little store by the idea that Douglas had not been in a mind to kill himself. He had certainly appeared depressed enough when Freddy had met him, and although Gertie and Tatty must have known Douglas better than Freddy had, he saw no reason to look beyond the obvious solution. Gertie's story that Douglas had found out something scandalous Freddy dismissed as being the product of her inaccurate recollections of that evening.

For the rest of the week he forgot about the matter, and went about his business as usual. On Saturday afternoon, however, he received a telephone-call from his father, to say had he remembered it was his mother's birthday tomorrow and that he was supposed to be coming to dinner? Freddy had, as he did every year, forgotten both of those things, and so he dashed out to Harrods to purchase a gift. Having completed his errand, he was just deciding to return home when he bumped into someone he knew. It was Lois Westray, accompanied by her step-daughter Alida Westray. Salutations were exchanged, and after some discussion they decided to go for tea in the Georgian restaurant.

'I say, I'm dreadfully sorry about Douglas,' said Freddy, once they had been seated.

'Yes, it has been rather horrid,' said Lois. Alida nodded in agreement. Her face looked a little drawn.

'Poor Father,' she said. 'He doesn't say much, but he's taken it very badly.'

'And what about you?' said Freddy. 'Are you all right?'

She gave a wan smile.

'I shall be, but one feels so helpless. If there were only something one could have done.'

Lois said:

'We had no idea he was so depressed. Of course, he'd had a few reversals lately, but they weren't anything that any normal young person couldn't have got over. He was only twenty-six, and had plenty of things to look forward to. It all seems such a terrible waste.'

'I don't think it's quite sunk in yet,' said Alida. 'I can't help thinking that he's going to walk through the door just as he used to. But he won't, will he?'

Freddy shook his head sympathetically.

'I'm afraid not.'

'And it's not just the death one has to get over,' said Lois. 'It's all the little irritations that go with it. Writing to the bank, and organizing the funeral, and replying to letters of condolence—that sort of thing. You'd think we didn't have enough to worry about, without everything else going wrong as well.'

'Why? What else has gone wrong?'

'Oh, just little things. Nothing important, but on top of all the other stuff it's horribly annoying. The police sent the wrong shoes back with Douglas's clothes, so we need to give these ones back and get the right ones. Lots of little things like that.'

'And his office at the factory was burgled too,' added Alida.

Freddy pricked up his ears.

'Burgled?'

'Well, not exactly burgled,' said Lois. 'Stanley says someone broke open his drawer. I assume it was a petty thief who got into the building when nobody was looking.'

'Was anything taken?'

'We don't know,' said Alida. 'It doesn't seem so. It's not as if he kept any money in there anyway.'

'But it's the kind of thing that gets Stanley terribly worked up,' said Lois. 'He sacked the porter, who was always letting people in when he oughtn't, and sent notes around to everyone telling them to be vigilant. I suppose it helps him—he's the sort of man who gets over things by keeping busy.'

'Look here,' said Freddy. I don't suppose anybody has suggested to you that it might have been anything other than suicide?'

The two women glanced at one another.

'Tatty said something of the sort,' said Alida at last.

'Tatty's upset about Doug's death, as we all are, and she's not thinking straight,' said Lois. 'Why? Has anyone else said anything about it?'

Freddy did not answer directly.

'It has been suggested that there may have been foul play,' he said carefully.

'You mean somebody killed him?' said Alida.

'Perhaps. I don't know. What do you think?'

'But he locked himself in,' said Lois.

'Yes, but it has been pointed out that since I got in through the window on the night I found him, someone else might have got in before me and escaped that way.'

They looked at him, open-mouthed.

'That's nonsense,' said Lois at last. 'Why, someone would have seen them, surely. Whoever it was would have had to come out along the fire escape and down the stairs, but people were up and down those stairs all evening. I know I was.'

'Did you see anybody?' said Freddy.

Lois blinked.

'Why, I—no, not that I remember. Did you go up there, Alida?'

'Yes,' said Alida. 'I went up there with Father. We both wanted a breath of fresh air, although there wasn't much of it there. That was early in the evening, before supper.'

'Do you remember seeing anyone else go up onto the balcony?' said Freddy. 'I mean to say, I don't suppose you spent the evening staring at the thing, but we were all in the garden for supper.'

They both thought.

'Lord Browncliffe, I think,' said Alida. 'And Tom and Tatty went up there as well.'

'When was that?' said Freddy.

'After supper. I remember thinking they both looked rather grim. It was after Doug had made an exhibition of himself during Lord Browncliffe's speech, and I assumed they'd gone up there to have it out.'

That agreed with what Tatty had told him. She had gone with Douglas into the smoking-room, and afterwards had had a row with Tom about Douglas's behaviour during Lord Browncliffe's speech.

'Listen,' he said. 'If you like I'll see about getting Douglas's shoes back for you. I'm in and out of police stations all the time in my job, so it won't be any trouble.'

'Oh, would you?' said Lois. 'I'd be awfully grateful. It will be one less thing to worry about, at least.'

So it was agreed, and soon afterwards they parted. Freddy decided that there was no time like the present, and since Scotland Yard was on his way home, more or less, he alighted there and asked to see Sergeant Bird. As it happened Sergeant Bird was in the office that afternoon, and was disposed to see him.

'Do you have any new information for us?' he said, when Freddy explained why he had come.

'No. I just wondered if I might have a look at the medical report. I don't suppose there's anything to find out, but I promised I'd look into it for a friend, so look into it I must.'

'A friend, eh? At a guess I'd say there's a lady in the case,' said Bird knowingly.

'There's always a lady in the case, sergeant,' said Freddy. 'But in this particular case, it's all quite above the board. I just want to assure her that everything possible has been done and nothing has been overlooked.'

'Hmm. So you want to see the medical report? As a matter of fact, I think I can do better than that.' The sergeant picked up the telephone and spoke into it. 'Ingleby's here this afternoon,' he said, as he replaced the receiver. 'He's the one who did the post-mortem examination on this chap. He'll be able to tell you anything you want to know.'

Dr. Ingleby arrived quickly, with his usual brisk manner, and asked how he might be of assistance.

'I have one question, and it's quite a simple one,' said Freddy. 'Are you absolutely certain that Douglas Westray died by his own hand? I know what they said at the inquest, but I'm talking purely about the medical side of things. Is it possible that someone else shot him?'

'If you're talking from a wholly medical point of view, then yes, it's possible that someone else shot him,' said the doctor. 'Of course it is—always assuming there were no witnesses to his death, which I understand there were not in this case.'

'No, there weren't. He was found with his arm dangling over the arm of a chair, and on the floor below his hand was a revolver. It looked as though he'd dropped the gun after he shot himself, but naturally it would be easy enough to stage an effect of the kind. Now, doctor, if someone had presented you with Douglas Westray's body without telling you the circumstances in which it had been found, what would you have thought? That is to say, would you have said without hesitation that he shot himself?'

The little doctor pursed his lips.

'Well, there are many factors to consider, you understand, although there are some things one can rule out. For example, he certainly wasn't shot from the other side of the room. To judge from my examination of the wound, I should say the gun had been held a few inches from the head before being fired.'

'A few inches? How many?'

'Difficult to say precisely. There was a certain absence of residue and burning on the skin of the deceased, which one might have expected from a gun placed very close to the temple. Taking that fact on its own I might have said the gun had been fired from perhaps six inches away.'

'Six inches? Isn't that rather far?' Freddy imitated the action of someone holding a gun to his own head. 'Wouldn't it be a strain on the wrist?'

'Perhaps. But I don't suppose the poor fellow was too concerned about a sore wrist at that moment,' said Ingleby dryly.

'Don't people normally hold the gun close to their temple when they shoot themselves?'

'They do, generally speaking,' agreed the doctor. 'But one never knows.'

'Then you wouldn't be prepared to say one way or the other whether it was his own hand that fired the shot, or someone else's?'

'I couldn't say for definite, no.'

'But it's possible that someone else *might* have done it?'

'That is so.'

He was evidently not prepared to commit himself any further than that, so Freddy gave it up. He thanked Ingleby and Bird, and was about to take his departure when he suddenly remembered his other errand.

'Oh, by the way,' he said. 'I've also come about Douglas Westray's shoes. It seems you chaps sent the wrong ones back to his family.'

'Did we?' said Bird, surprised.

'Apparently so. I said I'd collect the right ones, and I've no doubt that Lady Westray will send back the wrong ones in due course.'

There was some little delay while investigations were made, but at last Sergeant Bird came back into the office, frowning.

'Our chap says there's no mistake,' he said. 'Those are his shoes, all right. We haven't had anyone in wearing evening-shoes recently apart from Westray, so they can't have got mixed up with anybody else's.'

'Are you sure?'

'As sure as we can be. Renwick says there's no doubt those were the shoes he came in in, and they have no other shoes of that description among the lost property.'

'Odd. Perhaps Lois got it wrong, then,' said Freddy.

He bade the sergeant goodbye and set off for home, but he had not got very far before he changed his mind and decided he might as well stop at the Westrays' house on the way and inform them of the result of his visit to Scotland Yard. The Westrays lived on Brook Street. Freddy rang, and was informed that Lady Westray and Miss Westray had just arrived home. They were surprised to see him again so soon, and even more surprised when he explained why he had come.

'Oh, but there must be some mistake,' said Lois. 'They certainly sent the wrong shoes back.'

'Are you sure? How do you know?' said Freddy.

'Because they were completely the wrong size. I didn't look too closely at them myself, but Banning noticed and told me about it.'

'Banning?'

'He's Stanley's valet, but he also does—did—for Douglas sometimes. He's quite sure they're not Douglas's shoes.'

'Might I speak to Banning for a minute?' said Freddy.

'If you like,' said Lois.

Banning was summoned, and instructed to assist Mr. Pilkington-Soames in any way he could.

'Oh yes, sir,' he said, in answer to Freddy's inquiry. 'I noticed immediately. They certainly weren't Mr. Douglas's shoes. His were new, and quite different from the ones they sent back.'

'Might I see them?' said Freddy.

The man assented, and led Freddy upstairs and into what had been Douglas Westray's bedroom. Freddy looked around. None of Douglas's possessions had been cleared out yet, it appeared. Banning went across to a wardrobe and took out a pair of black dress shoes.

'These are the ones, sir,' he said.

Freddy took a shoe and examined it. It was quite ordinary—a plain men's dress shoe, Oxford style, in black patent leather with a toe cap, a little worn, and from its appearance, a few years old. He examined it closely, inside and out, but there were no distinguishing marks. He picked up the other shoe and examined that.

'You say Mr. Douglas's shoes were new?' he said thoughtfully.

'Yes, sir—never been worn until that evening, in fact. They were in polished box calf rather than patent leather, and in a smaller size. Mr. Douglas wore a size eight, and as you can see, these are a size ten.'

'Did you dress Mr. Douglas on the night he died?'

'Not to say dress,' said Banning, 'I helped him with one or two things, but he said he was in a hurry and would see to himself, so I said he might ring if he wanted me again, then left him.'

'He was in a hurry, was he? At what time did he go out?'

'At five o'clock, or thereabouts.'

'Wearing his own shoes, presumably.'

'Yes, sir.'

'How can you be sure of that if you didn't dress him?'

'Because I was arranging Sir Stanley's things in his room, which is just across the corridor. Mr. Douglas came out and asked if he should do, and I looked him over and saw that a scuff-mark had somehow appeared on his left shoe. He didn't want to wait while I polished it, so I rubbed the mark off as best I could and he went out.'

'Hmm. That seems clear enough. Five o'clock, though—that's rather early. He didn't arrive at the dance until nine, as I recall. Did he say where he was going before that?'

'Not that I remember, sir. I know he said he wanted to speak to a chap, but he didn't say who. I dare say he was meeting him at his club.'

'Which club is that?'

'Skeffington's, sir.'

Freddy thanked the man and returned downstairs, wrinkling his brow thoughtfully.

'Rather queer, what?' he said to himself. 'Why should Douglas change his shoes halfway through the evening? And where did he get the second pair?'

Chapter Eight

FREDDY WENT DOWNSTAIRS and found Alida sitting alone in the drawing-room.

'Anything?' she said.

'No,' said Freddy. 'Your man is quite certain that Douglas went out in his new shoes, and that the shoes which were sent back were not the same ones. The police are equally certain that they sent back the shoes Douglas was wearing when he was brought in, so we must assume that at some point that evening he changed his shoes. Any idea why that might be?'

'None at all. It seems very odd.'

'It does, doesn't it? Banning also says Douglas went out at about five o'clock, but he didn't arrive at the dance until quite late. Did he say where he was going?'

'Not as far as I know. I expect he went to his club.'

'That's what Banning suggested,' said Freddy thoughtfully, then took his leave and left. His curiosity had been well and truly aroused by this strange matter of the shoes, and he wanted to speak to Gertie about it, so he went to a telephone box and called her. A superior servant informed him that she was not at home, and he grimaced, for he was feeling too impatient to wait. There was nothing else for it: he would have to go to Skeffington's. It was a prospect which did not cheer him, for Freddy was a former member of that venerable establishment who was now something of a *persona non grata* there—indeed, not to put too fine a point on it, he had been ejected from the place on his ear for transgressions against decorum which still caused some of the older members to shudder at the memory, and which had led to the removal of all the stuffed animal heads from the walls of the library into the attics as a precautionary measure—and he was by no means confident that any of the staff would be prepared to speak to him. Still, the place was only a short walk away so there was no harm in trying.

Fortunately, the commissionaire was not one he recognized, and he was able to effect an entry without difficulty. His second stroke of good luck was to find on duty the assistant secretary, a man of less advanced years than the rest of the senior staff, and one who was inclined to look more indulgently upon youthful high-jinks than his superiors were. He opened his eyes wide when he saw Freddy.

'I say,' he said. 'You'd better not let old Calder see you. I've strict instructions to turf you out on sight.'

'You'd think he'd let bygones be bygones,' said Freddy. 'It was all a long time ago.'

'Less than a year, if we're counting.'

'Oh, but I've reached a maturer age now. I'm an old man of twenty-four and I can assure you I behave impeccably these days.'

'That won't cut any ice with him, I'm afraid. He's in a foul mood this week as it is. We had a leak from next door three days ago and the wine cellar was flooded. Six dozen bottles of Chateau Rauzan best claret and another four dozen of Martinez Old Tawny ruined, and who knows what else.'

'No!' said Freddy, shocked.

'I'm afraid so.'

They contemplated the tragic loss in a respectful silence.

'How can I help you?' hinted the secretary.

Freddy recollected himself.

'Just a little matter of business. I believe you have—or had, at least—a member named Douglas Westray. After my time, I think.'

The secretary's face clouded.

'Ah, yes, sad business, that. Suicide, I understand.'

'Perhaps. That's what I'm trying to find out. I gather he may have been here on the nineteenth of June, the night he died, and I'd like to speak to anyone who saw him.'

The secretary regarded him doubtfully. He was torn between duty and curiosity, but curiosity won the day.

'Stay here,' he said. 'And if you see Calder for heaven's sake hop it.'

He went away to make inquiries, and at length came back in company with one of the waiters, who suppressed a laugh when he saw Freddy.

'Sam here says he spoke to your chap on the night in question,' said the secretary. 'You may ask him, but let's go somewhere less public.'

They went into a private room, where the secretary could be reasonably sure that they would not be disturbed by the dyspeptic Mr. Calder. Sam was fortunately blessed with a good memory, and informed Freddy that Douglas Westray had arrived at Skeffington's at about a quarter to eight on the 19th of June. He remembered it particularly because Mr. Westray had glanced at his watch and mentioned the time when he arrived, saying that he could not stay long as he was expected at a ball he was not much looking forward to.

'That's nearly three hours after he left the house,' said Freddy. 'Was he sober?'

'Perfectly so when he arrived, although I shouldn't like to comment on his state after he left,' said Sam delicately.

'As bad as that, eh? What was he drinking?'

'He ordered several cocktails, then invited Colonel Lomas to join him in a drink. The colonel doesn't hold with cocktails, and so they changed to whisky at that point.'

'Is Colonel Lomas here now?' said Freddy.

'I saw him somewhere about,' said the secretary.

'I should like to speak to him if I may.'

'Listen, what's this all about? There'll be the most fearful row if you're caught.'

'I don't know exactly, except that there were one or two odd circumstances about Westray's death, and there's been some suggestion that it might not have been suicide, so I said I'd prowl around and ask a question or two. Now, Sam, I don't suppose you noticed Mr. Westray's shoes, did you?'

'No, sir. He was in his evening-things, but I didn't notice his shoes in particular.'

'He didn't, for example, take them off when he arrived then walk off with the wrong ones when he left?'

Sam stared.

'Not that I know of. I'm sure somebody would have mentioned it if he had.'

'Ye-es, I'm sure they would have. At what time did he leave the club?'

'Just before nine, sir. He asked us to get him a taxi and then he went off.'

'Very well, that will do for now.'

Sam was dismissed, puzzling over shoes, and Freddy was given permission to go and speak to Colonel Lomas, on the strict understanding that if Mr. Calder arrived he was to depart without fuss and must not, under any circumstances, mention that the assistant secretary knew anything about his visit. Colonel Lomas was eventually located in the bar, making obeisance to his fourth whisky and soda of the evening. He peered short-sightedly at Freddy, and was with some difficulty and the promise of another drink persuaded to cast back his mind to the night of the 19th of June.

'Ah—er—yes—Westray. Terrible business. Suicide, wasn't it?'

'That's what they said at the inquest, but we're just trying to make sure,' said Freddy.

'Felt very bad when I heard about it. Must have been one of the last people to speak to him. Wish I'd known—might have been able to say something to dissuade him.'

'He didn't say anything that suggested he was thinking of killing himself, then?'

'Not that I recall. Dismal enough, of course. Said he'd had the most awful day, and now he had to go and spend the evening at some ghastly dance or other when he wasn't in the mood. Talked about how chaps kept letting him down. First one, then another. And women, too. Well, I know all about that. Plenty of fish in the sea, I told him. One woman's much like the next. If one slips out of your hands it's easy enough to catch another. Trying to buck him up, you know.'

'He'd had an awful day, had he? Did he say why?'

'Well, I assumed he was talking about this girl, whoever she was.'

'I'm not sure it was that,' said Freddy. 'Do you remember his exact words?'

The colonel huffed and grumbled, but remembered the promised drink and tried to recall.

'He'd been talking to someone,' he said at last. 'He'd gone to consult a friend of his about something that was worrying him, but then he'd had a shock and had had to come away.'

'A shock? Did he say what it was about?'

'Not that I recall—ah, yes! He said that he'd had a double knock, and that it wasn't fair that everything should be laid on his shoulders when he had nothing to do with any of it.'

'Do you know what he was referring to?'

'I asked him, but he wouldn't tell me. He just said his faith in human nature had been shaken that day. "I can't decide whether or not to speak up, or whether to let sleeping dogs lie," he said. "If I speak up then it'll cause the most terrible stink—and what if I'm wrong? But if I don't then I'm party to murder, and I couldn't do that to the old girl.'

'Murder?' said Freddy. 'Are you sure that's what he said?'

'Oh, yes. I was as surprised as you are, and said so. That put the wind up him, and he begged pardon and said he'd misspoken, and that he'd been exaggerating. Then he started talking about honour and decency, and how there didn't seem to be much of it about these days. Of course, I know all about that. Chap ran off with my wife back in '99 while I was on my way out to Mafeking, and I never saw either of them again. Dreadful pity—I should like to speak to the man face to face, and shake his hand for doing me a good turn. Frightful harpy, she was. Never had a moment's peace. Pretty, though.'

He began to reminisce about the old days. Just then Freddy glanced up and saw the assistant secretary gesticulating frantically to him from the door and pointing behind him. Evidently Mr. Calder was on his way. He stood up and thanked Colonel Lomas, then made a furtive retreat from the club with the help of a marble bust of Caesar, which provided effective cover, and then through the cloak-room. When he got home it was nearly seven o'clock, and he decided to telephone Gertie again. This time she was at home.

'What have you found out?' she said.

Freddy told her about Douglas's visit to the club before he arrived at the Browncliffes' ball.

'So now we know where he went immediately before the dance, and where he got tight,' he said. 'But I'd like to know where he went between leaving the house and arriving at Skeffington's.'

'What does it matter where he went?' said Gertie impatiently. 'The time we're interested in is after ten o'clock.'

'It matters because of what you said. If he'd discovered something about someone—something that would provide a motive for his murder, I mean—then it's worth finding out whom he spoke to in the hours leading up to his death. Now, I spoke to an old duffer at Skeffington's who talked to Douglas on the evening he died, and he said more or less the same thing you did—that Douglas had been given a shock about something, and he didn't know what to do about it.'

'I knew it!' said Gertie triumphantly. 'You see? I wasn't just making it up.'

'It seems not. As a matter of fact, he went further and said that if he didn't speak up then he was party to murder, although afterwards he said he'd been exaggerating. Gertie, I don't suppose you noticed Douglas's shoes that night, did you?'

'Shoes? What a ridiculous question. Why on earth do you want to know about his shoes?'

Freddy explained.

'How very odd!' she said at last. 'Do you mean to say he exchanged shoes with someone? Might he have run home and changed them? Perhaps the new ones were giving him blisters.'

'No, they weren't his—Banning was quite sure of that. But you've given me a thought. If his shoes were so uncomfortable he couldn't bear to stand up in them, then perhaps he borrowed a pair from someone at the Browncliffes' house.'

'But from whom?'

'I don't know. Lord Browncliffe, perhaps? Who else was staying at the house that night?'

'Nobody, as far as I know. But they might have dug out a pair of old shoes from somewhere.'

'The question is, when did he change into them?' said Freddy. 'Do you remember whether he wearing his new ones at the dance?'

'No, of course I don't—oh!' Gertie thought for a second. 'Yes, I do,' she went on excitedly. 'He was wearing new shoes. He told me so. Not that I was interested, but he'd reached that stage of drunkenness in which one harps on about trivialities as though they're the most important things in the world. It was the first time he'd worn them, and they were very comfortable, he said. Then he started recommending the shop he got them from, and I pointed out that I was hardly likely to buy a pair myself, but he would keep talking about them and so in the end I was forced to kiss him just to shut him up.'

'Oh, so that's how you went about it. Listen, Gertie, could you call Tatty now and ask her to find out whether anybody in the house lent Douglas a pair of size ten shoes? I can't imagine Lord Browncliffe doing it, but one never knows.'

'All right,' said Gertie, and hung up. Fifteen minutes later she rang back.

'She hadn't the faintest idea what I was talking about,' she said. 'But I made her go and ask, and she came back and said all the men's shoes in the house are accounted for.'

'I see,' said Freddy. 'How very odd.'

'Which shoes was he wearing when you found him?'

'I only wish I could remember,' he said. 'I shall make further inquiries.'

'I dare say it's not important,' said Gertie. 'We'll probably find out there's quite a simple explanation.'

On the contrary, this was the first suspicious circumstance Freddy had discovered in his investigation so far, but he could not explain it. His thoughts were interrupted by Gertie, who had to go out.

'I'll speak to you soon, and we'll decide what to do next,' she said, then rang off.

As it happened, Freddy himself also had an appointment that evening, with a young lady. He went out and had a most pleasant time, and forgot all about Douglas Westray's suicide for a while.

Chapter Nine

IT SEEMED THERE was no answer to the question of what had happened to Douglas Westray's shoes; nobody could remember which shoes he had been wearing when he was found dead in Lady Browncliffe's dressing-room, nor was anyone able to shed any light on who was responsible for breaking into Douglas's drawer, since nothing was missing from it as far as anybody knew. Freddy therefore felt he had reached a dead end and could not proceed any farther in the investigation. Certainly, there were one or two queer circumstances surrounding Douglas's death, but those in themselves were not enough to point definitely to foul play, and in the absence of more evidence, Freddy concluded that it would be a waste of time to continue at present.

So Freddy put the thing out of his mind and turned his attention to other matters. July passed into August, and there were many public events which required his attendance for the *Clarion*. One of these was an air show at Heston, which was to be graced with the presence of the King and many great luminaries of the armed forces, particularly the Royal Air Force. A number of well-known names in the field of aircraft design and manufacture were to present their wares at the show, including Nugent Corporation and Westray Enterprises. Freddy was curious to see how they were all getting on since the death of Douglas Westray, so he took the assignment willingly when it was offered him and looked forward to a day spent in the open air in the pursuit of entertainment.

On the day of the show the weather was warm, clear and bright, with just the slightest touch of a breeze—perfect for flying, and for observing too. It seemed the people of London agreed, for they had flocked to Heston in their multitudes, attired in their best summer clothes, and were milling about the aerodrome, gazing at the exhibits as they waited for the air displays to begin. The exhibitors had erected large, white pavilions for the purpose of providing some respite from the hot sun, while stalls sold ices and lemonade and other comestibles, and the general air was one of festive enjoyment. When Freddy arrived he followed the stream of people who were heading as though drawn by a magnet towards the exhibits: a display of smart, shiny new aeroplanes, their paint gleaming in the sunshine. But there were so many people that it was difficult to get close, and so in the end he gave up and retreated towards a pavilion whose sign declared it to be that of the Nugent Corporation. There he found Gertie, wearing an enormous hat and a dissatisfied expression. She was attending the air show with her mother, the Countess of Strathmerrick, and was chafing under the necessity of being on her best behaviour. She brightened when she saw Freddy.

'It's awfully frustrating,' she said. 'I've been speaking to people all day, and nobody can help or tell me anything about Douglas. In fact, everyone seems to have practically forgotten him.'

'What do you expect? His death is over and done with officially. The inquest said it was suicide and there's no real reason to suppose anything different. To be perfectly frank I'm rather starting to come to that conclusion myself.'

'Oh but it can't be true,' said Gertie.

'Whether it is or not we've no evidence. I think perhaps you ought to let it lie, old girl. I know you feel bad, but he was responsible for his own actions.'

'I don't feel bad—I just know it wasn't suicide, I feel it in my bones. Well, if you won't help me I shall have to continue alone. Today is the perfect opportunity to speak to people who were at the dance, and that is what I intend to do.'

There was no arguing with her, so Freddy gave it up. He had a job to do in any case, and so he went off to do it. A little way from the Nugent pavilion, Lord Browncliffe was standing with Tom Chetwynd and a man of military bearing. Freddy approached with his notebook and an ingratiating air, and was introduced to Tom's father, Air Chief Marshal Sir Thomas Bryce Chetwynd, who was Chief of the Air Staff and a man of no little importance to the Royal Air Force, the British air industry, and himself. It appeared the Air Force and the Air Ministry were seeking to commission a new fighter plane, and Sir Thomas was attending the air show in his official capacity. His demeanour was stiff and reserved, and while there was some physical resemblance between him and his son, their characters were clearly very different. Tom Chetwynd the younger greeted Freddy's arrival with every appearance of relief, and took him to one side.

'All this business talk is a frightful bore,' he said in an undertone, 'but I have to take part and pretend I like it. Father wanted me to join the Air Force, you know, but I couldn't stand the idea. Now I suppose I'll have to come and work for Nugent Corporation after the wedding. I can't very well say no a second time, can I?'

There was a discontented look on his face as he said it.

'Aren't you interested in this sort of thing, then?' said Freddy.

'Not I! Far too many rules and regulations to remember. I spent some years out in Kenya as a boy, and I should have liked to go back out there and take up farming, but Father wouldn't hear of it, and I don't know whether it would suit Tatty. She'd have to leave all her friends.'

'So would you.'

Chetwynd gave a short, humourless laugh.

'What friends? I've no friends, and no-one to leave behind, not now—'

He stopped.

'You mean now Douglas has gone?' said Freddy.

'What? Oh, yes—yes. Poor old Doug. And poor old Tatty. She's been distraught about it, but can't tell me. It's perfectly obvious she was still in love with him, but it wouldn't be quite the thing to mention it, would it? Not now that we're supposed to be getting married.'

'Supposed to be?'

'*Are* getting married, of course. I gather the preparations are already under way, and we'll soon be quite the happy couple.'

There was a bitterness to his tone that he could not hide. Freddy raised his eyebrows but forbore to pry. He was remembering the night of the dance and the sight of Douglas squaring up to Tom and calling him an unprincipled bounder. Was that because Tom had taken Tatty from him, or was there something more to it? Tom had been upset and agitated that evening, even before Douglas had begun to cause trouble, so perhaps there was some other reason. He also remembered that old Colonel Lomas had mentioned that Douglas had gone to see a friend, and had received a shock. Was that friend Tom? Freddy was curious to know, but he could not think of a suitable way to introduce the subject, so he decided to leave it until another time.

The crowd around the display of aeroplanes was beginning to thin out, and so he wandered across again. Close to, the machines looked very fine, and Freddy admired the ingenuity which had gone into them. A whole display was dedicated to aeroplane engines and other components, and seemed to be presided over by Leslie Penbrigg, who was polishing the shiny metal surface of a large propeller with his handkerchief. At the end of a row of new aeroplanes stood an aircraft which was clearly much older. It was a Sopwith Camel, and here the crowd was larger. Freddy soon saw why, for standing by the plane was Captain Dauncey, who was laughing and evidently enjoying all the attention. According to a notice, the plane was the same one in which Dauncey had shot down so many of his German opponents during the war, and he was regaling his audience with tales of that time. Freddy stood for a minute or two and scribbled down a few notes, then began to observe the crowd. To his right a group of former servicemen were reminiscing about the war, and he listened with interest until they moved away. He noticed with amusement that the men in the crowd were mostly looking at the plane, while the women were mostly gazing, rapt, at Captain Dauncey. Freddy spoke to two gaudily-dressed young women who were enthusiastic in their praise of the great man, and the faded widow of an aircraft engineer who was scarcely less so, and who regretted the fact that her husband was no longer with them to see today's splendid exhibition, then he took some snapshots with his folding camera and wrote down a few notes with a view to composing a descriptive piece for the paper later on. He wished to take a photograph of Dauncey, but it was difficult to get close enough, so he turned his attention to the display of aircraft parts. The engineer's widow was also looking at the display, and was inclined to latch on to Freddy and talk at length about her husband. He had been a great one for inventing things, she said, and had left a whole notebook of ideas behind him when he died. Freddy got away from her at last and turned to see Gertie talking to Leslie Penbrigg, who, it seemed, was shy on all subjects except his job. When Freddy arrived Gertie was gazing glassily at Penbrigg as he described in great detail his latest work in the matters of crankshafts and engine mufflers and propeller reduction gears.

'There you are, Freddy,' said Gertie, interrupting Penbrigg rudely in the midst of a discourse on a new design of sparking plug. Penbrigg took the hint and coughed.

'Hallo, old chap,' said Freddy. 'Rather a jolly exhibition, what? You're here representing Westray, I take it? Are these all your inventions? Did you think of them all yourself?'

'What? Oh—er—mostly,' said Penbrigg. 'Of course, many of them are still in the early stages of development, but Sir Stanley wants to show the public the sort of thing we are likely to see in future.'

Freddy was about to ask a pertinent question about one of the devices on display, but Gertie evidently had other ideas and changed the subject abruptly.

'I don't believe we've seen you since the night of Tatty's ball,' she said. 'You remember, don't you? The night Doug died.'

If Leslie Penbrigg was disconcerted at this inelegant introduction of the theme he gave no sign of it. He looked grave, then took off his spectacles and polished them.

'It was a very dreadful thing,' he said soberly. 'It came as an awful shock to us all, and the family in particular. Nobody dreamed that he intended to kill himself.'

Freddy saw that Gertie was about to announce her suspicions to him quite openly and threw her a warning glance.

'Did you speak to him that night at all?' he said hurriedly. 'I mean to say, in view of what happened presumably you've thought back to the events of the evening. I know I've racked my brains as to whether Westray gave any hint of what he was planning to do, but I can't say he did—or not to me, at any rate. I don't suppose he said anything to you that night, or in the days leading up to his death?'

Penbrigg replaced his spectacles.

'No, certainly not. He'd been off work that week, and when he turned up at the ball it was the first time I'd seen him in days. I hadn't the faintest idea he was feeling so down. I'd have told them so at the inquest, but as it happens I wasn't required to give evidence.'

'How did Sir Stanley take his death?' said Freddy.

'Sir Stanley's one of the old sort,' Penbrigg replied. 'Doesn't like to show his feelings, but I imagine he was as upset as the rest of us.'

'*Were* you upset?' said Gertie bluntly. 'I understood you were angry with Doug because he lost you the Woodville Prize last year.'

Penbrigg looked blank, then comprehending.

'Oh, that. Yes, it was very unfortunate. I was a little annoyed at first, I won't deny, but he was so horrified and apologetic when he realized what he'd done—or rather, *not* done—that I told him not to worry. This business moves very fast, you know, and one has to be quick, or someone else will get there first.'

Freddy remembered his conversation with Alida Westray at the ball, when he had remarked upon the seeming coincidence of Nugent's and Westray's coming up with the same idea at once.

'Did it never occur to you that someone might have stolen the idea for the wing slots?' he said.

'What do you mean, someone might have stolen it?' said Penbrigg, startled.

'Well, it was rather a coincidence that Nugent just happened to think of the same thing at the same time as you, don't you think?'

'Oh—oh, yes, I see. As a matter of fact, I believe there was some suspicion that Douglas might have accidentally let the thing slip to the Nugent side when he was still engaged to Tatty. I know Sir Stanley thought so, although Douglas denied it. But I have no idea whether it was accident, theft or pure coincidence.' He shrugged. 'At any rate, Nugent won the prize.'

A muffled voice now issued from the loud-speaker just comprehensibly enough to communicate to them that the air display was about to begin, and the crowds began to drift down the airfield towards the runway. Freddy and Gertie followed.

'Hmph,' said Gertie. 'Far too good to be true!'

'What, old Penbrigg?'

'Who else?'

'You don't mean to say you suspect him?'

'Why not? He's the only person with any motive. He lost out on the Woodville Prize because of Doug, and he killed him for revenge.'

'Nonsense.'

'And he looked awfully shifty when he spotted you in the crowd, taking photographs.'

'Well, which is it? Too good to be true or shifty-looking? He can't be both at once. And in any case, why should the sight of me make him look shifty?'

'Because he knows you're a reporter and might dig up the truth at any moment.'

'I find your thesis unconvincing. Do you have any concrete evidence?'

'No,' admitted Gertie. 'I didn't see him up on the balcony that night, but that doesn't mean he wasn't there.'

'Well, then, if he did go up there, how did he get in through the window? He wasn't carrying a penknife.'

'He might have used something else. And besides, there's no reason to assume he got in that way. I thought we'd agreed the murderer might just as easily have gone through the door and come *out* through the window. If that's what happened, then he wouldn't have needed a knife. He could have just banged the window and the catch would have fallen down.'

They were passing the Nugent Corporation pavilion as she spoke, and they stopped as Captain Dauncey emerged from it, strapping on his helmet.

'Hallo, Freddy,' he said. 'Going to watch the show?'

'Rather. I say, may I have a photograph for the *Clarion?*' said Freddy.

'Certainly,' said Dauncey, glancing appreciatively at Gertie. 'Lady Gertrude, isn't it?'

'Gertie,' breathed Gertie, and just managed not to giggle.

Dauncey gestured to her to join him, and Freddy duly took a photograph of them both.

'What sort of display will it be, sir?' he said. 'Looping the loop, something of the sort?'

'Not exactly. It's to be a demonstration of the Nugent Nuthatch, Browncliffe's new fighter plane—I dare say you've read of it. I'm just going to put her through her paces, and show what she can do. There are some very earnest fellows here from the Air Ministry, and my job is to show them that the Nuthatch is the very plane they need. We don't want to be beaten by our rivals, do we? Westray and several other companies would like nothing better to get the business.'

'Do you think your plane will win?'

'Oh, we'll wipe the floor with them,' said Dauncey. He laughed, showing his white teeth. Gertie gazed at him adoringly. Freddy nudged her with his foot and she glared at him.

'Well, must be off,' said Dauncey. 'Don't want to start late.'

He gave Gertie a wink and strode off, the very picture of heroic manhood.

'Come on,' said Gertie. 'I want to find a good spot.'

Chapter Ten

THEY FOUND A place where a good view might be had of the runway, and Gertie raised a pair of field-glasses with which she had thoughtfully provided herself and began surveying the crowd.

'There's Mother,' she said. 'She'll be wondering where I am.'

She went off to join Lady Strathmerrick, and Freddy remained where he was. The first plane to take off was a Westray Ocelot, a wood-framed biplane, which, as far as he could understand from the dull honking and buzzing coming from the loud speakers, included something called an air-cooled radial engine and other features of an incomprehensibly technical nature. The machine zipped neatly along the runway and sailed into the air. It performed a series of daring rolls and loops, then came in to land lightly, to the sound of loud applause. It was followed by another aeroplane, produced by a different firm, which effected a number of exciting and dangerous dives, pulling up not fifty feet from the ground and rising back into the air. It was all very well done, and Freddy admired the engineering prowess which must have gone into producing such graceful, powerful machines.

He was watching the scene with interest and thinking of nothing in particular when he gradually became aware of a presence hovering at his elbow, and turned to see standing next to him a tall, thin young man upon whom Nature appeared to have bestowed more than his fair share of teeth and less than his fair share of chin.

'Well, if it isn't young Freddy!' said Corky Beckwith, affecting an expression of surprise. 'And what brings you here?'

'The same as you, I imagine—work,' said Freddy, for Mr. Beckwith was a reporter at the *Clarion's* rival newspaper, the *Herald*, and a perpetual thorn in Freddy's side.

Corky waved his hand and gave a heavy sigh.

'Yes, it's dreadfully unfortunate that one has to come to such places and mingle with the great unwashed in pursuit of an honest living. One had hopes of a preferment, but there was a little matter of a misunderstanding over my expenses. I told them the young lady was a valuable witness in a murder case, but they were unwilling to believe me.'

'You astonish me.'

'It was most provoking. They seemed to think it was a black mark against my character, which was infuriating enough, but worse than that, I was left severely out of pocket for the hotel bill and sundry other disbursements. So here you see me—' (here there was another sigh) '—toiling anew on my pitiful pilgrimage through the Slough of Despond, when I ought to have been celebrating my promotion to chief reporter.' He was patting his pockets as he spoke, and brought out a crumpled paper bag of confectionery, which he held out. 'Humbug?'

'Quite,' said Freddy.

Corky inserted a sticky-looking sweet into his mouth and gazed across to where Gertie was standing with her mother.

'I see you're here with Lady Gertrude McAloon. Any news you'd care to share?'

'What sort of news?'

'Oh, you know: engagements, elopements, that sort of thing. She's always good for a paragraph or two on a slow news day—all the McAloon girls are, in fact—but she seems to have been quiet lately. Any dirt there?'

'None that I'd be prepared to tell you.'

'Never mind. Whatever it is I shall find it out,' said Corky imperturbably, crunching his sweet.

'Or pluck it fully formed from whichever part of your body you're using for a brain these days,' said Freddy.

'You malign me unjustly, young Freddy. However, you are right in that one must allow oneself to use just a *little* poetic licence in these cases. The Muse must not be denied. Am I not as much an artist as Leonardo da Vinci or Michelangelo? Though of course we tread very different paths as we strive for mastery of our chosen fields. Man cannot live by mere labour alone, for he must have some kind of release for the fire of creation that burns deep within his soul, and whether it result in an exquisite form in polished marble to which thousands flock in order to admire, or a smartly-written piece in an organ sworn to uphold the national dignity, the spur is the same.'

'Look here, are you planning to go on all day? Because I'd rather like to watch the air show.'

'No, but seriously,' said Corky. 'As it happens, I'm not just here for the fun. What were you saying to Captain Dauncey just now?'

'Dauncey? We were talking about his plane. Why?'

Corky gave him a significant look and glanced around.

'Let's just say I'm doing a spot of digging at present.'

'Into Dauncey? What do you have?'

'You don't think I'm going to give away all my secrets, do you? But if you must know, I have it on very good authority that he's not quite the golden hero he's cracked up to be.'

'What makes you think that?'

'Well, it all started back in May, after he won the round-Britain air speed race. I dare say you remember it—there was some question as to whether all the contestants had flown the whole distance, and even a suggestion that *one or two* of them had sat out the northernmost leg of the journey and bribed the ground staff to keep quiet about it.'

'As I recall, nobody was suggesting that except the *Herald*.'

'Yes, rather a good idea of mine, wasn't it?' said Corky shamelessly. 'I worded it just vaguely enough so he couldn't possibly get us for libel. At any rate, I was looking for a pithy paragraph to finish my piece so I tracked him down to his club the day after the race, but I fear that he didn't take kindly to my presence and reacted rudely, not to say violently.'

'Oh? What did he do?' said Freddy with interest.

Corky pursed up his mouth primly.

'He kicked me in the—er—rear, and had me thrown out of the club. It was a terrible thing. Just imagine treating the press like that!'

'Au contraire,' said Freddy. 'Why the devil wasn't he immediately knighted by a grateful nation?'

'Aha! But that's exactly my point,' said Corky eagerly. 'The whole episode started me thinking. Why *wasn't* Dauncey given a knighthood after the war? Or a statue, at least. Do you know how many German planes he shot down? Thousands! Or lots, anyway,' he amended, on seeing Freddy's face. 'And then he slunk out of the flying corps with nothing more than a handshake and a few medals. I suspect there was some dishonourable behaviour there, but it was never made public because of his heroism during the war.'

'Your imagination is a rich and fertile place,' said Freddy.

'Scoff all you like, but I scent wrongdoing, and my nose has never yet led me astray. However, once again I find myself thwarted by my humble antecedents and lowly birth—I went to the wrong school, you see, and so nobody will speak to me.'

'Nobody will speak to you because you're an ass. It has nothing to do with the school you went to.'

'Once again you exult over your social inferiors even as you grind them under your heel. I suppose I oughtn't to have expected anything more of you, but I did think you might be prepared to help a fellow press-man.'

Freddy's curiosity got the better of him.

'What exactly do you suspect him of?' he said.

Corky glanced around again and lowered his voice.

'For one thing, nobody seems to know where he gets his money from. You must have seen how he lives: a flat in town, all the finest restaurants, champagne, clubs, racing cars, planes, the lot. Now you can't tell me he affords all that from his paltry wages as a test pilot.'

'Perhaps he has a private income,' suggested Freddy. 'Lots of people do.'

'He hasn't—or not one that I've been able to discover, at any rate. He comes from a modest family and has no property or inheritances to speak of, and yet he wallows in the lap of luxury among all you lot.'

'Well, then, I expect he's in debt.'

'Hmph. No more than you are,' said Corky. 'I tell you, he's up to his neck in some dirty business, and I mean to find out what it is.'

'Do you have any proof of this, or is it just another wild product of your fevered brain?'

'Oh, well, if it's *proof* you want, then I can't help you,' said Corky. 'Isn't my word enough for you?'

'No.'

'Then I take it you're not interested in sharing the scoop with me.'

'You don't have a scoop. All you have is a half-baked idea that someone you don't like is up to no good. Show me some solid evidence and I might take you seriously, but until then you can forget it.'

'Pleased with yourself as usual, aren't you? But you'll see I'm right. Who was right in the Dacres case?'

'Not you,' said Freddy.

Corky ignored him, and went on knowingly:

'Just you have a word in Dauncey's ear and see what he says. And don't forget to let me know. This could be a huge story for both of us if you've only the wit to follow my lead.'

He strolled off and Freddy shook his head. He was convinced that Corky's view of Captain Dauncey was strongly coloured by vindictiveness. He turned his attention back to the air show, in which a display was taking place of a new kind of passenger aircraft which was meant to have the most comfortable cabin yet seen in any aeroplane. After that there was a short interlude of formation flying by a group of trick pilots. He had been shielding his eyes with his hand, but the sun was beginning to make them water, and so he looked away for a few moments and saw Tatty Nugent approaching him. She still wore the sad, anxious expression he had seen on her the last time they had met. It was hardly an appropriate look for a young woman who was soon to be a bride, and he supposed she was still mourning Douglas. She soon confirmed his guess.

'I don't suppose you've anything to tell me?' she said in a low voice. 'About Doug, I mean.'

'I'm afraid not,' said Freddy. 'As far as anybody is aware, Douglas's death was exactly as it appeared to be: an unfortunate suicide. Sorry, old girl, but without any new evidence there's not much else I can do.'

'That's a pity. Did you ever find out what happened to his shoes?' she said.

'No. That was a queer circumstance, right enough, but I can't see where it fits into the affair at all.'

'Nor can I, and I've tried and tried. I only wish I knew exactly what happened that night. Isn't there anything you can think of that might help us?'

'You might give me a little information. I don't suppose it has anything to do with the thing, but what can you tell me about Captain Dauncey?'

'Captain Dauncey?' she said in surprise. 'I don't know much myself. He's a good friend of Father's, though, and it was a great coup for Nugent to get him as a test pilot. He got along very well with Doug, too.'

'Did he, indeed?' said Freddy, pricking up his ears.

'Oh yes. They were very pally at one point and went out together often. I wasn't especially keen on it, to be perfectly honest. Dauncey moves with a fast crowd, and they all tend to drink too much. That's when Doug started doing it, to try and keep up, and you saw yourself how good he was at holding his drink.'

'That is to say, not very.'

'Exactly. And there were other things that went on. I think they gambled a lot—cards, mostly, but horses and motor-races too. Of course, they were rather thrown in each other's way when Doug and I were engaged, so I expect that's why they palled up.'

'And did they remain friends after you broke off the engagement?'

'Why, I—' she stopped to think. 'Now you come to mention it, things had cooled between them, but it started a while before Douglas and I parted ways.'

'Oh?'

'Yes, it must have been last year, around the time that Nugent Corporation beat Westray Enterprises to the Woodville Prize, and poor Douglas was getting the blame for it from all sides. He was very grumpy at the time and not exactly good company, so perhaps that's why Captain Dauncey gave up on him.'

'Ah, yes, the wing slot patent. I think there was some question as to whether Douglas might have accidentally let slip the information about the invention to you.'

'He certainly didn't!' she said emphatically. 'He was always very scrupulous about that sort of thing—and in any case, there would have been absolutely no use in his talking to me about it, because I don't understand aeroplanes and never shall. I felt dreadfully sorry for him, because his father refused to believe he hadn't done it.'

Freddy was thinking. He had not been aware of Douglas Westray's friendship with Captain Dauncey, but it seemed to shed a new aspect on the case. Might Douglas have found out something to Dauncey's disadvantage which required him to be put out of the way? Freddy could not help remembering that Dauncey had been carrying a penknife on the night of the dance, with which he could have opened the sash window from the outside. Was that what had happened? Had Dauncey gone up the fire escape, seen Douglas through the window and seized the opportunity to get in and murder him? But no—that was not possible: he could not have seen Douglas, because the dressing-room curtains had been closed. Freddy shook himself. It was all pure speculation at present, and all because Corky had a bee in his bonnet as usual. Would the idea have even occurred to him had Corky not piqued his curiosity about Dauncey's past? Most probably not.

The next person to speak to him about Douglas was Lois Westray, who was wearing an anxious expression not dissimilar to Tatty's. Freddy congratulated her on the successful performance of the Westray Ocelot.

'Yes, it went rather well, didn't it? I'm glad for Stanley, since he hasn't had much to celebrate recently. With any luck this will bring in some new business and help him get over what happened. Not that money is any sort of compensation for Doug, but at least it will keep his mind off things.'

'Did he take Douglas's death badly, then? He doesn't seem the sort to show it.'

'He isn't, but that's just his manner. He really was dreadfully cut up about what happened. Despite everything he was very fond of Douglas.'

'But wasn't he disappointed in him for losing Tatty and all the business that might have come his way through a closer partnership with Nugent?'

'Yes, but he'd have come round sooner or later. It's all too late now, though.' She seemed agitated about something. 'Listen, I've been thinking about what you said the other week about Doug's death, and its not being suicide. Do you really think it's true?'

'I don't know. I suppose it's just possible that somebody might have got into the room, killed him, then come out through the window, but whoever it was would have been taking an awful risk—I mean to say, there were hundreds of people milling about that night, and he might have been seen.'

'Oh, but you see, he wouldn't,' she said. 'It's occurred to me that if somebody did come in or out through the window then there's a very good chance he wouldn't have been seen at all.'

'Why's that?'

'Because of the lights. Don't you remember? The terrace was lit up so brightly that it threw everything else into shadow, and at least one of the lights was placed just below the balcony and directed towards the terrace. I remember it particularly, because I came out to look for Stanley at one point, and when I looked up at the balcony the light below it quite blinded me, and I couldn't see a thing.'

'I believe you're right,' said Freddy, considering. 'It was mid-summer, so light for most of the evening, but it would have been dark enough by ten o'clock. You went up there after supper, didn't you?'

'Yes, but I hope you don't think I had anything to do with it!'

'Of course not, but perhaps you might have seen someone up there at the same time.'

'No, I saw no-one.'

It was the second time she had denied seeing anyone on the balcony, but Freddy remembered that part of the evening very well—and also remembered that Lois had come down the fire escape only a minute or two before Captain Dauncey, and so must have seen him up there. He wondered why she was lying about it.

Chapter Eleven

DAUNCEY'S PLANE WAS now taxiing along towards the runway in preparation for take-off, and the chatter in the crowd swelled as the excitement mounted. The other displays had been all very well, but the Nugent Nuthatch was the real star of the show, for the Nugent Corporation—and Lord Browncliffe in particular—had been busy over the past few months seeking publicity for the machine, and instilling in the minds of the public the idea that it would be the next great aircraft—the fighter of the future, able to hold its own in combat should the unthinkable happen and war break out again. The crowd were therefore eager to see the first public appearance of this great national feat of engineering, flown by Captain Dauncey, the great national hero.

The loud speaker was informing the crowd indistinctly of the Nuthatch's technical particulars. It was a two-seat, twin-engined monoplane constructed all in metal, with a top speed of almost two hundred and fifty miles per hour, and contained no less than twenty-one patented inventions. The speaker droned on, but few were listening, for they were all preoccupied with the sight of the plane itself as it stood poised at the end of the runway, preparing for flight. Heads strained to see above the crowd, and the shorter people stood on tiptoe, trying to catch a glimpse of Captain Dauncey, whose head was just visible in the cockpit, clad in its leather helmet. The propeller whirred, then hummed as it spun faster and the plane moved forward, gaining speed as it went. It lifted lightly and smoothly into the air, and there was a sigh from the crowd as Dauncey immediately began putting the plane through its paces. He ran it back and forth across the aerodrome once or twice, then took it a little higher and performed a series of rolls and other aerobatic manoeuvres which demonstrated its capabilities to a marvel. This was quite obviously a much sleeker and better plane than any of the others on show, and the crowd were enthralled. The Nuthatch disappeared into the distance, and the observers waited on tenterhooks for it to return, wondering what it would do next. They soon found out: a tiny speck appeared in the sky, growing larger and larger by the second, then there was a huge roaring overhead and it vanished into the distance again as the crowd gasped, and the loud speaker honked out a speech of which the only words which could be distinguished were a startled 'My word!' and 'tremendously fast speed!'

Having demonstrated how fast the Nuthatch could go, Captain Dauncey then slowed and began a rolling circuit of the aerodrome, turning from side to side, then finally performing a full roll before righting the plane and climbing steeply, almost vertically, many hundreds of feet into the air. The aeroplane slowed as it climbed, then at the very pinnacle seemed to stop and hang motionless in the air, tail downwards, for several seconds. Then slowly the nose of the plane turned towards the earth and the Nuthatch went into a dive, descending at a rate that was almost a free-fall. For several seconds it looked as though the plane and Captain Dauncey would plummet into the ground, but at the last moment he pulled the nose up again and swooped low over the airfield. The crowd roared its appreciation, and the Nuthatch once again began to climb, presumably to repeat the manoeuvre. This time, however, it got no farther than a few hundred feet from the ground when it gave a great lurch and a cough, and began to twist oddly. Something had clearly gone wrong. Dauncey abandoned the manoeuvre and somehow managed to right the plane, to cheers from the crowd, who evidently thought it had all been intentional. The Nuthatch flew level, circling the aerodrome for some minutes, then began to climb again. Once again, however, the plane stalled and jerked, and began to behave even more erratically than before.

'What the devil is wrong with that plane?' muttered Freddy to himself. He looked around, wondering whether he was the only one to have noticed, and saw that some people had begun to look worried. Corky Beckwith was standing nearby, watching eagerly and taking notes. He glanced at Freddy's folding camera with envy.

'I wish I'd thought to bring one,' he said. 'Just imagine if I captured the moment it hit the ground!'

Under normal circumstances Freddy would have replied with some caustic remark, but his eyes were drawn irresistibly to the scene in the sky above him. Dauncey was fighting to regain control of his aircraft, but it was refusing to obey his command.

'Good heavens, he really is going to crash!' said Corky, with barely-concealed delight. Indeed, the Nuthatch appeared to have declared independence from its pilot, and looked as though it wanted nothing more than to point itself towards the earth and embark upon a catastrophic nose-dive. With a superhuman effort Dauncey managed to keep the nose up, but the plane was still descending dangerously fast. The crowd had at last realized that something was very wrong, and there were screams and shouts as the plane picked up speed, heading directly for the pavilion section of the field. Down, down, down it came, and the crowds around the pavilions began to scatter and run in all directions. Calamity seemed inevitable, and Freddy was just about to close his eyes, when at the very last second Dauncey somehow regained control of the machine, and it roared low over the aerodrome, just missing the roofs of the pavilions. Dauncey made sure the plane was straight, then finally brought it down into a bumpy landing and drew it to a stop. The crowd erupted in cheers and cries of relief, although Corky was looking disappointed.

'So much for the Nuthatch,' he said. 'Perhaps the famous Captain Dauncey isn't quite such a whiz at flying as we all supposed. Or perhaps it's the plane that's a dud. I shall go and take a closer look.'

He went off, but Freddy did not follow him, for it was obvious that the public would not be allowed near the thing—and indeed, the Nuthatch had already been wheeled to the side of the airfield, and was surrounded by engineers. After a few minutes another aeroplane took to the sky, and Freddy scribbled down one or two notes, but in reality he was looking about for Lord Browncliffe or Captain Dauncey. It looked rather as though Browncliffe's hopes of selling the Nuthatch at a pretty price were doomed to failure—at least until it could be ascertained what had gone wrong with it—and the events of today would make a good story, especially if Freddy could speak to any of the men involved to find out what had happened.

At length Lord Browncliffe strode back to the Nugent Corporation pavilion, in company with Captain Dauncey. They were met by a group of their own people, and there was much conferring in murmurs. Lord Browncliffe had invited a number of official guests from England and abroad to watch the display, and after a minute or two Freddy heard him raise his voice.

'No, no, just a little trouble with the engine,' he said jovially to one of his visitors. 'Nothing at all of importance. It seems one of the fuel lines was badly fitted, but I shall find out who did it and have some sharp words with him. Yes, it is rather vexing, of course. Makes a bad show, especially on its first day. Just a little stumbling-block—or let's call it a dress-rehearsal. Yes, a dress-rehearsal, that's what it was. Went a little badly, but these things often do. But we're taking her down to Shoreham-by-Sea for the South of England air show in a couple of weeks, then you'll see what she's capable of!'

Hands were shaken all round, and two of the foreign guests departed, glancing at one another and grimacing. A few minutes later Freddy noticed them looking around the pavilion of a rival company, Rawson Welbeck, where a smiling man greeted them. Lord Browncliffe had nothing to do now but swallow his irritation at what had happened and appear with all his usual bonhomie—a feat he managed with some success until he saw Sir Stanley Westray approaching, with Lois following a little way behind, looking slightly apprehensive. Sir Stanley, it seemed, had come to satisfy his curiosity as to what had gone wrong with the Nugent Nuthatch, but had not the finesse of manner required to do so diplomatically.

'What went wrong, Browncliffe?' he said bluntly. 'Wasn't the plane ready yet? I thought you said you'd ironed out all the remaining problems. It looks as though you missed a few.'

Lord Browncliffe drew himself up.

'The plane was in perfect condition this morning. It was examined by three of my best mechanics. There was nothing wrong with the thing then. I wonder, though—perhaps you can explain who cut through the fuel line to the left engine, because Dauncey tells me that *someone* certainly did.'

'I beg your pardon?' said Sir Stanley, taken aback. 'Do you mean to say it was cut deliberately? Why, that's sabotage!'

'Indeed it is, and I shall be reporting it to the police! Somebody attempted to ensure that the Nugent Nuthatch would make a miserable showing at today's air display—presumably in order to ruin its chances of success, given that it's far and away the best fighter aeroplane in existence today—and I mean to find out who it was!'

'But why are you asking if I can explain it? Are you suggesting that *I* had something to do with it?'

'Well, did you?'

Sir Stanley spluttered.

'Certainly not! This is outrageous, and tantamount to slander, and in front of witnesses too!'

'Nonsense! I never said you did it, merely asked if you did.'

'Naturally I should never dream of such a thing! How could you possibly insinuate that I should stoop to sabotage? If anybody is engaged in underhand methods I should say rather that it was Nugent Corporation. You may boast that you won the Woodville Prize on merit, but there are some who know the truth. What do you say to that, eh?'

The two men were puffed up like pigeons, glaring at one another. Fortunately for decorum, however, their respective wives were signalling to one another and preparing to intervene.

'Walter, dear, here's Mr. Dupont wanting to speak to you,' said Lady Browncliffe. 'Don't keep him waiting.'

'Now, Stanley, you know you said you would speak to the man from the Ministry shortly,' said Lois. 'He's in the pavilion, probably wondering where you are.'

So Lady Westray and Lady Browncliffe coaxed their husbands away from each other, and the onlookers breathed sighs of relief—or, in the case of the ever-present Corky Beckwith, pouted with disappointment that the two men had not come to blows. A brass marching-band now came on to provide entertainment, while the crowd ate ices and drank lemonade and enjoyed the music. The near-miss in the air was forgotten, and Captain Dauncey was seen out and about signing autographs. The official story was that it had all been part of the performance, aimed at demonstrating how the aeroplane responded in emergencies, and Dauncey was laughing easily and shrugging off all suggestions that his life had been in peril at any time.

The afternoon was wearing on, and Freddy began to think about leaving before everybody else had the same idea. He saw Tatty standing alone by the Nugent pavilion and felt sorry for her. He still had no idea whether Douglas's death had been suicide or murder, but he resolved to have one last try for Tatty's sake. Perhaps somebody could explain the matter of Douglas's shoes, if only to remove one niggling point in the investigation. To that end, he sought out everyone he knew to have been at the dance and asked them the question, but all reacted with surprise, even incredulity, and nobody seemed to know what he was talking about. Lord Browncliffe in particular looked at Freddy as though he thought he were imagining things, but after a moment suggested that since the boy had evidently been in a state of mind in which his sanity was disturbed, there was no saying whether he might not have taken it into his head to go out into the street and exchange shoes with some stranger. This was patently nonsense, but Lord Browncliffe had no other suggestion to make. Captain Dauncey looked equally blank, as did Leslie Penbrigg and Tom Chetwynd, so Freddy gave it up. He spent some time taking photographs, and was preparing to take his departure when he spotted Corky Beckwith talking to Gertie, who was regarding him with some aversion.

'Is this a friend of yours?' she said as Freddy approached. 'He says he is.'

'Nothing could be further from the truth,' said Freddy. 'Hop it, Corky, there's a good chap.'

'This is a public event, and I'm entitled to stand wherever I please,' pointed out Corky. 'If Lady Gertrude finds my company unpalatable, then she has only to move away and find a more pleasant vantage point.'

'I've already tried that, but you followed me,' she said.

'Only because you wouldn't answer my question. If you'd give me a quote, or something I could use, then I'd leave you alone.'

'But I don't have anything to tell you. I'm here with my mother, watching the air show.'

'Come, now! The fabled Lady Gertrude McAloon with nothing to tell? The same Lady Gertrude who not so long ago was fined twenty pounds for assaulting a police officer with a dangerous weapon and bound over to keep the peace for six months?'

'Oh, yes, I did do that, didn't I?' said Gertie, struck. 'I'd completely forgotten about it. That was a fun night. Anyway it wasn't a dangerous weapon, it was a sausage. Still, it's not the sort of thing I make a habit of, so I'm afraid you're wasting your time today.'

'What, not even an engagement to announce? You and young Pilkington-Soames here seem to be getting along rather well.'

He was eyeing them as he spoke, for Gertie was indeed at that moment clinging to Freddy's arm in a most familiar manner.

'Don't be—' began Freddy, but Gertie had suddenly perked up.

'I have no idea what you're talking about,' she said, then fluttered her eyelashes at Freddy and kissed him on the cheek with a giggle. 'Let's just say I have nothing to announce at present. Come along, Freddy.'

She dragged Freddy away from Corky, who was looking as though he had just been told he was to receive his promotion after all.

'What was that for?' hissed Freddy.

'I was just trying to get rid of him,' said Gertie. 'It worked, didn't it?'

'But he'll never let me alone now. The man has been put on this earth purely to plague me, and now he'll be even worse.'

'Oh, bother, you're no fun,' said Gertie. 'One day I shall find a man who can take a joke and I'll marry him so fast he won't know what's hit him.'

Freddy had no time to reply, because just then Lady Strathmerrick approached and informed Gertie that it was time to go home, and the next few minutes were necessarily taken up with polite nothings. The two ladies went off, and Freddy decided to follow suit. He took an underground train into London, and stopped at the offices of the *Clarion* in order to write up his notes quickly. It was half past six by the time he had finished, and he came out onto Fleet Street, musing pleasantly over how to spend the evening. As luck would have it, he was perambulating idly towards home when he bumped into an old friend of his, whom he had not seen for many years, and who, as it turned out, had embraced the law as a profession and had just been called to the Bar. There was much shaking of hands and clapping on the back, and after a very few minutes it was decided that the street was not the most suitable place in which to exchange all the news, rumour and gossip that each man harboured within him, and so they repaired to a local hostelry for their greater comfort.

There was much to hear and relate, and evening had lengthened into night and light faded into darkness by the time Freddy emerged from the drinking establishment and set off the few hundred yards for home, not entirely steady on his feet, but by no means incapable. He strolled through the narrow streets of Chancery Lane, enjoying the clement night air and the unaccustomed quiet of the city, which was broken only by the low hum of a nearby motor-car travelling at a slow speed somewhere behind him, then emerged on to Fleet Street and stepped out into the road in order to cross. What occurred next Freddy was never quite sure; all he knew was that it happened very quickly. He was aware of the sudden revving of an engine, and turned to see a long, dark shape hurtling out of the street from which he himself had just emerged and approaching him at speed. It had been driving without head-lamps on, but as it turned towards Freddy these were suddenly illuminated, almost blinding him. The motor-car was not ten yards away from him, and it was accelerating rapidly. Freddy had no time to think before it bore down upon him. There was an instant of panic, then he dived to the left—not quite quickly enough, for the car caught him a glancing blow as it passed, propelling him into the path of a taxi which was travelling in the other direction. Fortunately, the taxi-driver screeched to a stop just in time. He alighted from his cab in great indignation.

''Ere, what's all this, then?' he said. 'What do you think you're doing, throwing yourself in front of a man's car when he's going about his lawful business?'

Freddy was lying sprawled and dazed in the street. He raised his head and stared blearily at his accuser.

'That car,' he said weakly.

The taxi-driver turned, but the car which had done the damage had roared off into the night, and there was no possibility of getting another glimpse of it.

'It's gone,' said the driver. 'Did he hit you?'

'I—I—' Freddy was trying to sit up, and at length managed it. He felt his limbs and his head gingerly. There seemed to be nothing broken, but there was a nasty rent in his jacket, and another in his trouser leg. The speeding motor-car had hit him only in passing, but he had grazed himself badly when he fell. He examined his hands, wincing. They were scraped and sore.

'You're bleeding,' observed the taxi-driver. He had evidently decided that Freddy had not thrown himself in front of his cab merely to cause him inconvenience, and his manner softened somewhat. 'You all right?'

'I think so,' said Freddy, although he was by no means sure that this was the truth.

'Here.' The driver stepped forward and helped him up. 'People want to be more careful. Some of these drivers nowadays are a menace.'

'Did you see the car?' said Freddy.

'No. It all happened too fast, didn't it? If he'd had his headlamps on in the first place, like what he oughter, he'd have seen you sooner and been able to stop. You want to get off home and get yourself bandaged up. Can I take you anywhere?'

'No—no, thanks. I'm just round the corner.'

'Well then, don't stay out here and wait for someone else to run you down,' said the taxi-driver, then got back into his car and drove off, comfortable in the knowledge that he had done his bit.

Freddy was feeling dazed, a state which had nothing to do with how much he had drunk that evening. Somehow he made it back to his flat and examined himself in the glass. He was a sorry sight indeed: the fall had taken a patch of skin off his cheekbone just below his left eye, and he had grazes on his hands and knees. In addition to that his right leg was feeling very painful from where the car had glanced against it, and he could feel bruises beginning to form on several other parts of his body. He cleaned himself up as best he could and bandaged the worst of the grazes, then collapsed into bed. But he did not fall asleep immediately; instead, he lay awake for some time, staring into the darkness and wondering just who it was who had tried to kill him, and why.

Chapter Twelve

ON MONDAY MORNING, Freddy arrived at the *Clarion's* offices at about a quarter to ten—a not unusual time for him—and sat down at his desk. Jolliffe was sitting nearby, frowning over his notebook.

'Morning,' he said, without looking up. 'How was the air show? Bickerstaffe's given me this story about traffic management and congestion, and too many cars trying to leave the show at once on Saturday—you know, after that woman was knocked down and killed. I don't suppose you saw anything of it and can offer an opinion?'

'No,' said Freddy. Jolliffe looked up and gave a start at the sight of him.

'Good Lord! What on earth have you done to yourself? Have you been fighting again?'

Freddy winced. His bruises were in full bloom now, and he was quite a sight.

'No—as a matter of fact I was hit by a car.'

'You too? There seems to have been quite an epidemic of it at this air show. I'm rather glad I missed it.'

'It wasn't at the air show. It was at about half past eleven on Saturday night when I was on my way home.'

'Ah, Saturday night, was it?' said Jolliffe, a look of comprehension crossing his face, for he knew Freddy's habits only too well. 'I expect you'd had one over the eight, had you? Still, there's no reason for anyone to go mowing a chap down with a motor just because he's had a drink or two.'

'I was perfectly sober, as it happens—well, near enough. I was fully *compos* at any rate.'

He related the bare facts to Jolliffe, who commiserated and went back to his work, leaving Freddy to ponder. He had been in too much pain for most of Sunday to think clearly or come to any conclusions, but things were easing somewhat (here he touched the graze on his face, which was crusting over nicely), and it was time to do some reasoning. First: could he be sure the incident on Saturday night had been deliberate? Might it not have been an unfortunate accident? To this the answer was surely no. For one thing he had heard the car following him for some way before it happened. He had not thought anything of it at the time, but now it looked as though the driver had been waiting for his chance, which had come when Freddy turned into Fleet Street. For another thing, the mysterious driver had switched on his lights only at the last minute, presumably to dazzle and confuse his quarry. Furthermore, he had speeded up as he approached, and then afterwards had driven off without even stopping to make sure Freddy was not injured. No, it had certainly been deliberate. That led to the second question: why? Freddy could think of only one reason, and that was the fact that he had asked all the people who had been at both Tatty's ball and the air show whether they knew anything of Douglas Westray's shoes. Had anybody's reaction to the question been suspicious? Freddy thought back, trying to picture the faces of the people to whom he had spoken, but was forced to admit that they had all looked completely blank. He had no idea what it all meant, but one thing of which he was becoming increasingly sure was that he had frightened someone into trying to kill him because he had been asking questions about Douglas's death—and the only logical conclusion to draw from *that* was that Gertie and Tatty were right, and his death had been murder.

He was still pondering the question when his editor, Mr. Bickerstaffe, came in and regarded him with horror, and he was once more required to give assurances that he had not been fighting. Mr. Bickerstaffe looked unconvinced, but let the matter drop and gave him a story which took up all his concentration for the next few hours, so he was forced to abandon the question of his attempted murder for the present. By three o'clock he had completed the assignment to his and Mr. Bickerstaffe's satisfaction, and was able once more to turn his attention to the cause of his bruises. After some reflection he called Gertie and hinted that he had something to tell her. She was most put out that he refused to explain himself over the telephone, but her curiosity was piqued, and she agreed to meet him for tea at the Lyons'.

'Good gracious! What *have* you done to yourself?' was her first remark when she arrived and found him nursing a cup of tea and an indifferent-looking slice of cake. 'Have you been fighting again?'

'Why does everybody seem to think I like nothing better than to hurl myself gaily into any wild free-for-all I happen to stroll past?'

'Because you do,' she said.

'You wound me, child. At any rate, it's not true—especially this time.'

He explained what had happened, and she forgot her tea and listened, enthralled.

'Well!' she breathed at last. 'I knew it! There's a killer on the loose! Are you quite sure you didn't see who it was?'

'No—the head-lamps were shining in my eyes and I couldn't see a thing. I couldn't even tell you whether it was a man or a woman.'

'And you've no idea what kind of car it was?'

'No. It all happened far too quickly, and it had disappeared before I could collect my thoughts together.'

She thought.

'How can we find out who it was? I suppose the quickest and most efficient way would be for you to do exactly the same thing again—you know, go around asking questions and hinting that you think it was murder, so as to try and draw him out and have another shot at killing you.'

'Kind of you to volunteer me as bait for a murderer's trap, but I'll stay out of it if it's all the same to you.'

'But we must do something! Don't you see? This is the first real evidence we have that Douglas didn't kill himself. Have you reported it to the police?'

'Of course not. What could I say? That I'd been weaving my way gently home after one or two stiff ones and almost came a cropper while crossing Fleet Street, but I can't tell them what sort of car it was or who was driving, or even be sure it was deliberate?'

'When you put it like that it doesn't sound exactly convincing,' she admitted. 'Well, then, we must look into it ourselves. Give me your notebook and a pencil. How shall we start?' She thought a minute, then began writing busily. 'I'm just putting down a short description of the circumstances of Doug's death. There! Now, let's make a list of suspects.'

'But how do we know who to suspect when we don't know how it was done?'

'I thought we'd decided the murderer got out through the window. I showed you, remember? The catch closes by itself if you give it a bit of a rattle.'

'Ye-es,' said Freddy. 'But if you recall that's only because I loosened it when I went in. And it doesn't close all the way.'

'Do you have a better idea?'

'No.'

'Then let's assume for now that that's what happened. Very well, taking as read that the murderer escaped by means of the window and the fire escape, who are our suspects, and what are their motives? First, Leslie Penbrigg. He has the most obvious motive—at least that we know of. Douglas lost him the Woodville Prize and he wanted revenge.'

'But he's mooning around Alida,' said Freddy. 'Killing her brother is hardly going to endear him to her, is it?'

'Of course he didn't think he would be found out. But leaving motive aside, *could* he have done it? Did you see him up on the balcony that night?'

'He was up there for a while earlier in the evening,' said Freddy, thinking. 'But that was when Douglas was still tottering around the garden making a nuisance of himself. The time we're interested in is after supper, when it was dark and the lights were switched on. Unfortunately, once that happened it was almost impossible to see who was up there.' He told her Lois's observation about the terrace lights. 'So you see, after about ten o'clock nobody could have seen what was happening on the balcony. Anyone going up or down the stairs would have been visible, but once they were up there they might have done anything and nobody would have known, as long as they were alone up there.'

'Then we must find out whether anybody saw Penbrigg go up there after supper,' said Gertie, looking at her notes. 'But how do we do that? There were hundreds of people milling about and we can't go around questioning all the guests.'

'What about the servants who were standing at the table? As I recall some of them were there for most of the evening, facing the balcony. Perhaps they'd remember who went up the stairs.'

'Good idea,' said Gertie. 'I shall put that down under the heading "Actions." Very well, who's next? Now it gets more difficult. Who else had a motive? I mean to say, I know Doug could be an ass at times, but he wasn't the sort of person people hated.'

'Tom Chetwynd.'

'Not the Chetwynd boy! I won't believe it. He's dim, but a darling. Why have you fixed on him? He had no motive at all for it.'

'He did have a motive—he was worried his girl was going to leave him for Douglas, and so he put a stop to it before she could do it.'

'Nonsense.'

'Not at all—don't you remember what Tatty said? Someone overheard her in the smoking-room, telling Douglas that she would consider going back to him, and Tom was standing outside in the hall when she came out. And he was carrying a penknife big enough to take the whole window out, let alone lever the catch up. He might easily have done it. And Alida saw him go up on the balcony with Tatty after supper.'

'But that would make Tatty an accomplice.'

'Well, isn't it possible? Perhaps after they talked in the smoking-room she decided Douglas was too much of a nuisance, and so she and Tom put their heads together and cooked up a daring plot to get him out of their hair.'

'Don't be ridiculous,' said Gertie, although she was considering as she spoke. 'She can't have been in on it, or she wouldn't have been so keen to insist it was murder. She was still sweet on Doug, I'm sure she was.'

'So she says. But she knew where the guns were kept.'

'Everybody knew where the guns were kept. There was a big piece in the *Tatler* a few months ago about Lord Browncliffe and his dratted gun collection, with a photograph of him next to his gun cabinet. Anybody could have gone in and helped themselves. I don't know why he didn't keep the thing locked.'

'I expect he will from now on,' said Freddy dryly. 'As a matter of fact, I agree with you. I don't think Chetwynd and Tatty did it between them, but Chetwynd is hiding something, I'm sure of it.'

'Oh? Explain.'

Freddy told her about Tom Chetwynd's agitated manner on the night of the dance, and about Colonel Lomas's story.

'And I've just remembered something else,' he said. 'He dropped a letter and I picked it up for him. He was pretty keen to shove it back in his pocket, but I shouldn't have thought anything of it had he not said it was from his mother.'

'What of it?'

'I got a good look at the envelope when I was handing it back, and saw it had been posted in Henley.'

'Of course it had,' said Gertie. 'That's where his people live.'

'But he said it was from his mother *in France*. His parents were abroad at the time and couldn't come, don't you remember?'

'So they were.'

'The letter was in a woman's handwriting, but it wasn't from his mother, that much I'm sure of,' said Freddy.

'That doesn't mean he was up to something. I dare say it was something quite innocent,' said Gertie.

'Then why lie about it?'

'There you have me.'

'I don't know how it all fits into this case, but I should very much like to know what Tom Chetwynd is concealing, and whether Douglas knew about it.'

'All right, I'll put him down,' said Gertie reluctantly. 'Although I don't know how we're supposed to find out this secret of his, short of wrestling him to the ground and stealing that letter off him.' She scribbled a note. 'Now, who else?'

'What do you think about Browncliffe himself?'

'As the murderer? Why?'

'If we assume he was the one who overheard Tatty and Douglas in the smoking-room—remember, Tatty said she saw Tom talking to her father when she came out, so it might just as easily have been he who was listening—then he might have taken fright at the idea of Tatty's taking Douglas back, and decided to take matters into his own hands.'

'To the extent of murder? Do you think he was so keen for Tatty to marry Tom that he was prepared to kill someone?'

'It doesn't seem likely, does it? But I suppose one never knows. If Tatty marries Tom Chetwynd, who's the son of the Chief of the Air Staff, then there are very valuable government contracts to be had from the connection. If she'd married Douglas there would probably have been a merger between Nugent and Westray sooner or later, but that wouldn't have been nearly so lucrative as the business they could get from the Air Ministry—or so satisfying from Lord Browncliffe's point of view, given his personal rivalry with Sir Stanley. I expect Browncliffe was much keener to have a leg-up with the Ministry than he was to form a partnership with Westray.'

'Hmm,' said Gertie, and made a few notes. 'Is that everybody? What about Alida and Sir Stanley and Lois?'

'Alida and Sir Stanley did go up on the balcony for a while, Alida says, but that was before supper, and we don't have enough evidence or a strong enough motive for either of them to have done the murder. Sir Stanley wasn't too pleased with his son, but I can't see why he'd want to murder him.'

'No, I can't either. All right, I'll put their names down with a question mark, until we find out more. Who else?'

'What about Dauncey?' said Freddy tentatively.

'What? Why in heaven's name would Captain Dauncey want to kill Doug?' said Gertie.

'I don't know, exactly, but I gather from Tatty that they were friends at one time.'

'I didn't know that.'

'Yes. Tatty said Dauncey runs with a fast set, and had lured Douglas into playing cards and drinking heavily, and all that sort of thing. I've also heard one or two things about Dauncey's money, and suggestions that his funds are not gained entirely honestly, let's say.'

'No!' said Gertie. 'Where did you hear that?'

'I have my sources,' said Freddy mysteriously. He was not about to give Corky the credit if he could help it.

'Do you think Doug had found out something about him and so Dauncey put him out of the way?'

'It's a flimsy theory, I know, but it's all I can think of.'

'We do rather seem to be clutching at straws on some of these motives,' she said. 'Still, we must do what we can. Let's look at the facts. Might Captain Dauncey have killed Doug? Did he go up on the balcony that evening?'

'Yes, he did. I saw him myself, coming down the stairs some time after supper.' He did not mention that Lois had been there at the same time, for he was at a loss to explain that matter. It might easily have been perfectly innocent, except that Lois had denied seeing Dauncey up there. Gertie was no fool, however. She narrowed her eyes.

'You've got that funny look you get when you're not telling me everything,' she said. 'Come on, out with it.'

'Oh, very well,' he said, and told her about Lois coming down from the balcony shortly before Captain Dauncey. 'She's told me twice now that she didn't see anyone up there, but she must be lying. It wasn't possible to see who was up there from the ground, but one couldn't stand on the balcony without noticing someone else was there.'

'But this is important! Why didn't you mention it before?'

'Well, you know, it was none of my business, and I do have my gentlemanly moments.'

'But what if she was telling the truth?' said Gertie excitedly. 'What if she was up there and didn't see Dauncey because he wasn't on the balcony at all? What if he was in Lady Browncliffe's dressing-room killing Doug, then came out of the window after she'd gone and followed her down the steps a few minutes later?'

Freddy considered the theory. It certainly had possibilities.

'He did have a penknife on him,' he said. 'But as you so rightly point out, that might not be relevant. He could have gone into the dressing-room through the house, after going into the library to get one of Lord Browncliffe's guns.'

'Yes, then he locked the door, shot Doug, and got out through the window just after Lois had gone. I expect he waited for her to go away before he came out.'

'It makes sense as far as it goes,' he said. 'But if Lois was up there while Dauncey was in the dressing-room, then why didn't she hear the shot? And what about the shoes and the other things? Where do they come in?'

'What other things?'

'The bent pen nib and the broken comb.'

'Oh, those,' she said dismissively. 'They're not important, are they? Anyone might have done that. It was probably the servants, as Lady Browncliffe said.'

Freddy was not convinced. He was almost sure there was some reason for the pen and the comb that he had not yet understood.

'I'd like to have another scout around Lady Browncliffe's dressing-room,' he said at last. 'I can't help thinking I must have missed something the first time I looked around. I should like to absorb the atmosphere and let it inspire me to genius.'

'Oughtn't we to be investigating Captain Dauncey instead? Shall I tackle him? Perhaps I can persuade Father to invite him to dinner,' she said hopefully.

'No, leave him alone—there's not much use in your talking to him. I'd better speak to him myself.'

'What do you mean there's not much use in *my* talking to him? I can be every bit as charming as you when I like, and I'm much prettier, too. I could smile winningly at him and ask him all sorts of pertinent questions.'

'About what, exactly? His financial affairs, and where he gets his money? How do you propose to introduce that subject? "Oh, Captain Dauncey, is it true you made your fortune in stocks? If so, I wonder whether I could tap you for advice. Canadian

Pacifics were down five-eighths yesterday and I was wondering whether I ought to get out and dive into Molasses instead." He'll think you're one of these female intellectuals who reads the newspapers and can discourse knowledgeably on the ins and outs of the Anglo-Afghan Treaty.'

'The what? Oh, very well, then, I suppose you're right. I can't exactly ask him where he gets his money. But you must let me speak to Lois, woman to woman. If there's anything questionable going on between her and Captain Dauncey then you can be sure I'll find it out.'

'All right, but for God's sake be diplomatic.'

'Hmph. I am the very soul of diplomacy. And don't look at me like that! I can be awfully discreet when I want to be.'

'I'll take your word for it.'

'So, then,' went on Gertie, looking at Freddy's notebook. 'We have a plan of sorts. You shall go and snoop around Lady Browncliffe's dressing-room with a magnifying-glass and a yard measure, and I shall speak to Lois and find out what exactly she did on the balcony that night, assuming it's fit to tell. I rather hope it isn't—I've been so fearfully well-behaved myself lately that I crave excitement in the form of indecorous behaviour from others. Then after that we'll compare notes, and then decide what to do about Dauncey. Now, anything else?'

'Not that I can think of,' said Freddy, although in actual fact his mind had wandered back to the air show, and the disastrous exhibition of the Nugent Nuthatch. Had it really been sabotage, as Lord Browncliffe had claimed? He had been angry at the time, and looking for someone to blame, so perhaps he had exaggerated in the heat of the moment. However, he had certainly mentioned a cut fuel line, which did not sound like an accident or negligence. Assuming it was sabotage, then did it have any connection with Douglas Westray's death? Freddy could not see how the two events were linked, but it was yet another odd fact among a series of odd facts. The more he looked into this strange affair the more complicated it seemed to become. He had nothing except the vaguest of suspicions at present, so he said nothing about the supposed sabotage to Gertie, and the two of them parted, having agreed to meet again once one or other of them had some news to tell.

Chapter Thirteen

AFTER LOOKING AT his watch, Freddy decided it was too late to go back to the office, and that he might be more usefully employed in some other activity. To that end, he decided to walk from Fleet Street to St. James's Square, and consider the facts of the Westray case as he went. Although he was now sure Douglas Westray had been murdered, he was forced to admit they still had very little evidence of anything; moreover, there was a good chance no further evidence would ever be found, and that the mystery would remain unsolved. The thought of this irritated him—not, truth be told, because of his burning desire to seek justice for Douglas, but because his bruises were still aching and the graze on his cheek still smarting from his narrow escape of Saturday night, and the idea that whoever had tried to run him down might never be caught filled him with indignation. So as he walked he revolved the case in his mind, and thought back to the evening of the dance, trying to remember the arrangements, and how people had looked and what they had said, but without reaching any useful conclusions. At last he turned into St. James's Square, stepped up to the front door of Badenoch House and rang the bell. The *Clarion's* own social page had told him that the Browncliffes were not at home, having gone down to Cowes for a day or two to watch the regatta, and so he hoped to be able to investigate freely without having to waste time in polite conversation with Tatty or Lady Browncliffe. Nobody answered for several minutes—presumably along with the Browncliffes had departed all sense of urgency—but eventually the door was opened by a smart maid, who informed him that the family were not at home.

'Yes, I know that,' said Freddy. 'As a matter of fact, it was you I wanted to speak to. It's Mabel, isn't it?'

'Sally, sir,' said the maid in surprise.

'Ah, of course. You'll remember me—at least, I hope so. I'm a friend of Miss Nugent's, and I'm here about the death of her young man—or perhaps I should say her *former* young man, Douglas Westray.'

Sally's eyes brightened at the prospect of news to share with the rest of the servants.

'Oh, yes, sir, it was a terrible thing to happen. Poor Miss Patricia, and she couldn't say a word because she's engaged to another gentleman now.'

'I suppose not. It wouldn't look too good to be seen to be mourning too deeply, what? Listen, do you mind if I come in?'

She stepped back and let him into the hall, glancing around nervously as she did so. Freddy guessed she did not wish to fall foul of the butler or the housekeeper.

'Now, I don't know whether Miss Patricia has mentioned it at all,' he said, 'but there are one or two queer circumstances surrounding Mr. Westray's death, and I said I'd look into them. As you know, he was found dead in Lady Browncliffe's dressing-room after a dance that was held here on the nineteenth of June.'

She shuddered.

'Yes, sir. Horrible, it was. None of the servants can bear to go in there any more after what happened—and neither can her ladyship.'

'So I understand. All her things were brought out and the room was locked up, I gather.'

'That's so.'

'Very good. Now, here's where you might be able to help me. Did her ladyship happen to mention a broken hair-comb to you?'

'A broken—' she stared at him in astonishment. 'Why, yes, she did, now I come to think of it. She thought I'd done it, but I hadn't.'

'Are you quite sure of that?'

'Of course I am—I mean, yes sir. I told her it was already broken when I brought it out of the dressing-room.'

'And what about Mabel? Might she have done it?'

'You can ask her, but her ladyship's already spoken to her about it and she says she never did it either, and it's not fair on us to keep saying we did.'

Her manner was a touch heated. Freddy hastened to reassure her.

'Naturally I shouldn't dream of accusing you. I'm merely trying to find out how it got broken—or if not how, then at least when. I don't suppose you recall when you last saw it in one piece?' She was shaking her head, and he went on persuasively, 'Now do try and remember. It might be awfully helpful to Miss Patricia.'

'All right, then, let me think,' she said. 'I know it was still in one piece the day before the ball, because her ladyship was thinking of wearing it that night. She tried it on, then took it off again and said it was too old-fashioned.'

'And did you see it again after that?'

'Not so as to notice it.'

'And the next time you saw it, it was broken?'

'That's right, sir.'

'Now, there's also the little matter of a twisted pen nib. Has her ladyship mentioned that?'

'The gold one? Now, that is a strange thing, sir, because her ladyship says she wrote a letter with that very pen not an hour before the ball began, and it was working perfectly then. But who would have picked the pen up after that? Nobody would have used it while the dance was going on, and then afterwards—' she shuddered again. 'No-one wanted to go into the room at all once Mr. Westray had been found there. Here, it's Mabel.' Freddy looked around and saw another maid peeping curiously around a door. She whisked out of sight when she saw him looking, but Sally called after her, 'Mabel, this gentleman has come to ask about what happened at the ball. Come out, won't you?'

Mabel reappeared shyly, and Freddy repeated his questions, but she had no more idea than Sally did about what had caused the damage to Lady Browncliffe's things. Just then, Whitcomb the butler turned up and began to reprimand both of them for idling.

'I beg your pardon, it was entirely my fault, Whitcomb,' said Freddy. 'I had a question or two to ask them, and they've been most helpful.'

The maids were sent off, and Freddy explained the situation. Whitcomb appeared uncertain as to whether stiffness or amenability were required of him, but once Freddy had assured him that Miss Patricia had particularly asked him to look into the thing, he decided in favour of the latter and softened somewhat.

'May I help at all, sir?' he said.

'As a matter of fact, I was hoping to speak to some of the servants, to ask whether anyone saw anything of what happened that night. I was thinking in particular of the ones who were standing behind the buffet table in the garden. I want to know who went up onto the fire escape, you see,' he explained, 'and since the table was facing the direction of the stairs, perhaps one of them might have seen something.'

'Lady Browncliffe has taken most of the kitchen staff down to Cowes with her, as she needs them for a large dinner-party,' said Whitcomb, 'so I am afraid it will not be possible to ask them.'

'That's a pity,' said Freddy. 'I wonder—might I go into the garden for a moment?'

After a moment's hesitation the butler assented, and led him through the ballroom and into the garden by way of the

French windows. Freddy went across to stand where the buffet table had been set on the evening in question, and immediately saw that it was no use, for the branches of a large tree, hanging over the wall from the garden next door, almost completely obscured the view of the fire escape stairs from that part of the terrace. This was a blow, for he had been hoping that an eagle-eyed servant might have been observing the comings and goings, but there was little use in asking them now, for if the tree branches blocked the view in daylight, it would have been even worse in the dark.

'I see I'm wasting my time,' he said. 'I say, Whitcomb, I don't suppose you'd let me have another look at Lady Browncliffe's dressing-room, would you? Is it still locked up?'

The butler replied in the affirmative and went to fetch the key. The room was even dustier than it had been three weeks ago when Freddy had last seen it, but otherwise nothing had changed that he could see. The pen lay on the blotter where he had left it, and he went across and stared at its twisted nib. Then he went to stand in the middle of the room and gazed around, trying once again to see in his mind's eye how the room had looked the night he had found Douglas Westray lying sprawled in the chair, dead. Something had been out of place then. What was it? He closed his eyes and pictured the scene. He thought it was something near the door.

'The plates,' he said suddenly. The butler looked at him inquiringly.

'I beg your pardon, sir?'

Freddy went towards the door and looked at the china plates which hung around the wall.

'There was a gap on the wall, just here I think,' he said, indicating. 'The night we found Douglas, I mean.'

The butler's face cleared.

'Yes, sir. One of the plates fell down on the night of the dance. I don't know how it happened—I thought at the time that the reverberation from the gunshot must have knocked it off. It was on the floor just here, so I put it back up.'

'When was this?'

'After you entered through the window and let us all into the dressing-room, sir. Everyone was crowding around poor Mr. Westray, so I thought I had better keep out of the way, but I stood near the door as I was sure that I would most probably be wanted. That's when I noticed the plate had fallen down, so I picked it up and hung it back on the wall. Luckily the carpet is soft so it was not damaged at all.'

'Which plate was it?'

'This one, sir.'

Freddy gazed at the plate. It had gilt edging and a pattern of leaves and flourishes painted in gold against a vibrant blue background, with in the centre a hand-painted arrangement of colourful flowers. He reached up and took it carefully down from the wall, to which it had been attached by means of a brass wire plate-hanger and a hook in the wall. He peered closely at this hook for some minutes, then turned and spent a little time considering the door. After that, he bent down and squinted at the keyhole, then stood up again, slid the bolt of the door backwards and forwards a few times, and at last went out into the corridor and regarded the door from the other side. Then he came back in, went across to Lady Browncliffe's sewing-box and poked about inside it.

'Might I help in any way, sir?' said Whitcomb, agog with well-bred curiosity.

'I don't think so,' replied Freddy, slamming the lid of the box shut. 'I've seen everything I need to see, thank you.'

He picked up the plate from where he had rested it carefully against the wall and put it back where he had found it, thanked the butler, then went away, thinking very hard.

Chapter Fourteen

MEANWHILE, GERTIE WAS chafing with impatience at her forced inactivity. She had taken on the task of speaking to Lois Westray, but on inquiry it turned out that Lois and Alida had also gone down to Cowes with Sir Stanley, and so she was left with nothing to do except wait for Freddy to call. Waiting was not something Gertie did well—and moreover, she was irritated at Freddy's casual supposition that she had neither the brains nor the qualifications to interview Captain Dauncey—and so she set herself to thinking about how she might effect a meeting between herself and that gentleman, in order to put some discreet questions to him. She came up with several ideas, each one wilder than the last, but none was suitable or practicable, and in the end she discarded them all. Had Dauncey been a young man of her own sort it would have been easy enough, for there were any number of places where they were almost certain to meet, and she would merely have arranged to bump into him and then manoeuvred him into asking her out for dinner; but it did not do for a young lady of noble family to chase after older men of unknown reputation—at least, not publicly, and while sober—and so she was forced to think of another means to her end. She knew the clubs he was supposed to frequent, but those establishments were denied her, and she could not spend her days hovering around Pall Mall in the hope of seeing him, so how could she hope to speak to him?

In the end she resorted to the simplest solution, which was to look up his address in the telephone directory, and to her great satisfaction she found that he lived in a flat on Bruton Street, just around the corner and not thirty seconds' walk from Bond Street. There was every reason in the world for a young lady of noble family to be seen drifting idly up and down Bond Street for hours at a time, and so Gertie decided to do exactly that for a day or two, in the hope of seeing him—for surely he must leave his house occasionally, and when he did she would be looking out for him.

So it was that on Tuesday morning Gertie sallied forth from the Strathmerrick residence in Grosvenor Square, with the purported intention of buying a new frock. She was careful to take a route which went along Bruton Street, and slowed down as she passed the entrance to Captain Dauncey's building, but to her disappointment there was no sign of him. She glanced at her watch. It was only half past nine, and not to be supposed that a man who was known to keep late hours would be up yet, so she passed on and turned into New Bond Street, where she spent the next hour pleasantly occupied in matters of a feminine nature, and spent rather a lot of money. In between visits to shops she took care to make regular forays into

Bruton Street, but there was still no sign of Captain Dauncey. She began to worry that she might miss him, but she could not very well loiter about outside his house without drawing notice, and so there was nothing to do except return to Bond Street. This time she wandered up and down, staring fixedly into shop windows without going in, and glancing frequently towards Bruton Street, but still she did not see him. By lunch-time she was tremendously bored; she had been into every purveyor of fashionable and expensive ladies' attire within a hundred-yard radius, and some of the newer shop-assistants who did not know who she was were starting to give her suspicious looks. Moreover, she had not eaten since breakfast and she was starting to feel hungry.

'Bother!' she muttered to herself. 'And to think reporters spend all day waiting about for things to happen. I don't know how Freddy does it. Well, I can't stand it. I'm going home, and I shall just have to think of another way to meet him. Oh, but there was a hat—'

The next fifteen minutes were given over to the purchase of a few scraps of silk and ribbon which would undoubtedly earn her a breathless paragraph in the social pages of the *Clarion*, but which would certainly not be proof against the slightest puff of wind or drop of rain, then Gertie emerged, having instructed them to deliver the hat to Grosvenor Square, and satisfied that she had achieved *something* that day, at least. Then her heart gave a great thump, for there he was—Captain Dauncey, just crossing the corner of Bond Street, but instead of coming out of his house he was heading towards it. She must have missed him that morning, and now he was coming home for lunch.

She was about to dive across the road after him, but found her way blocked by a group of elderly women, who seemed to be engaged in a competition to see which of them could walk the slowest. Gritting her teeth, she waited for them to pass, and hurried along Bruton Street just in time to see Dauncey disappear through his front door. This was all most vexing, and she stood and fumed for several minutes until she realized there was no sense in waiting, since he was obviously going to have lunch before he came out again. In frustration she returned to Bond Street and entered another shop in which she had seen a frock she had half-thought of buying. Ten minutes later she was standing in front of a looking-glass, draped in silk and stuck full of pins, when to her horror she saw in her reflection the unwelcome sight of Captain Dauncey walking past the shop window.

'Rats!' she exclaimed.

Gathering up her borrowed skirts, she ran towards the door, and would certainly have hurtled down the street after him had not the shop-girl put a stop to it. With an exasperated groan Gertie hurried back into her own clothes, threw the frock at the startled girl and ran out. Alas, Captain Dauncey was already a hundred yards away, striding purposefully along Conduit Street, dashing all her plans of pretending to encounter him by chance. She ran after him as far as Regent Street, where he turned left, heading towards Oxford Circus, and then prepared to descend into the Underground station. At that, Gertie brought herself up short. Why exactly was she following him? Had she managed to bump into him 'accidentally' then she might have fallen quite casually into conversation with him—

even gone to lunch with him—and perhaps learned something useful. But chasing him across London was another thing altogether, and she had no good explanation for it if he happened to turn around and see her. It was a futile endeavour, and she would be much better off returning home and leaving Freddy to tackle him.

She had just come to this conclusion when Captain Dauncey stopped to one side of the entrance to Oxford Circus station to light a cigarette. As he did so he glanced about, and there was such a furtive, guilty look about him as he did so that Gertie was quite startled. Quick as a flash she made up her mind and dashed after him as he entered the station. Inside the ticket-hall it was very crowded, which allowed her to get closer to him without being spotted. He purchased a ticket to Liverpool Street, and she did likewise, then followed him down onto the Central London line platform. A train was just drawing into the station, and she debated for a second whether or not to get into the same carriage as Dauncey, but decided against it—crowded as the place was, there was still a risk that he would see her—and got into the next one instead. Then the train pulled away and she immediately regretted it. What if he changed his mind and did not get off at Liverpool Street after all? The idea of losing him after all her trials of the morning was insupportable, and at every stop she jumped up and peered out through the door to make sure he had not got off, earning herself some odd looks from the other passengers. At Liverpool Street she leapt out, and to her relief saw him moving through the crowd on the platform to the exit. He emerged into the open and set off down the street, his pursuer keeping a discreet distance behind him. Gertie looked about her as she walked. This was an area of the city with which she was unfamiliar, and she felt a little nervous, since the people hereabouts were not of the sort with whom she was accustomed to mix. As far as she could tell, they were heading further East, and she began to wish she had worn more sensible shoes, for she had been on her feet all morning and they were beginning to ache. This part of town was run-down: they were not yet quite into the East End, but in an area in which businesses of the less salubrious sort seemed to operate, and Gertie suddenly realized that she ought to pay more attention to where they were going, for if she lost sight of Captain Dauncey, she would have great difficulty in finding her way back again. A pair of rough-looking men eyed her up and down most impertinently as they passed, and she was sure one of them muttered something disrespectful, although she could not hear exactly what he had said. Perhaps Freddy had been right, and she ought to have left well alone.

She had just begun to make up her mind to look about for a taxi and return to the safety of the West End, when she saw Captain Dauncey slow down at last and turn into a shabby-looking office building. She had taken refuge in a doorway as she saw him turn, and she waited a few minutes in order to make quite sure that he would not come straight out again, then approached the building cautiously. A faded name-plate affixed crookedly to the wall outside informed her that these were the premises of the Stamboul International Export Co. Gertie hesitated a few moments, then took a deep breath and pushed the door open. She had no idea what she would say if

Dauncey were just behind it, but she had come too far to back out now, and she was alive with curiosity. Fortunately, all that was behind the door was a dingy entrance-hall, containing only a small table on which a good deal of post had piled up. Gertie glanced at one or two of the envelopes, but none of the names were familiar to her, and several of the letters had been marked with the words 'not known at this address.' The entrance-hall ended in a flight of stairs, and she ascended them cautiously, thankful that her footsteps made no noise on the dusty carpet. At the top of the stairs was a corridor, at the end of which was a glass-panelled door, slightly ajar, through which she could hear the sound of voices. One was low and foreign-sounding, while the other was Dauncey's. He sounded quite unlike himself, his voice hard and contemptuous. Gertie stood and listened.

'—and you can tell him it's the last time,' Dauncey was saying. 'I've had enough of it. It's sick-making, d'you hear?'

'You are paid well for it,' replied the other. 'Do not think we are unaware of the life you lead. We know very well that you enjoy the finest things, and have women looking at you and the nation adoring you. What more do you want?'

Dauncey gave a sardonic laugh.

'I want my honour back. I'm sure I used to be an honourable man once, many years ago, but look at me now. What have I become? A coward, who does things he despises because he can't see another alternative. Well, this is the last time—I want no more of it!'

'So you think? We shall see what Mr. Salmanov says,' said the other man.

Dauncey said something unrepeatable, and Gertie blinked.

'Still, you will not turn down your payment, I think.' The other voice had a mocking tone to it.

'You think it's funny, do you? Be careful, or one day I might lash out, and then you'll be smiling on the other side of your face.'

The foreign voice hardened.

'You tell *me* to be careful? Then I tell you the same thing. You would be wise not to test me. I am not so stupid as not to provide myself with a weapon.'

'Oh, so that's the way it is, is it? I suppose I oughtn't to be surprised that someone of your kind feels the need to carry one of those around with you. But don't worry—you've nothing to fear from me.'

'Then *you* have nothing to fear from *me,*' said the foreign man politely.

The voices diminished to a murmur, then a chair scraped and the sound of approaching footsteps could be heard. Gertie, caught off guard, leapt back and whirled around, looking for somewhere to hide. A few feet away was a window recess, across which a curtain was almost fully drawn. She darted into it, and immediately discovered she was not the only occupant. She jumped violently and only just managed to stop herself from giving a shriek of terror.

'Why, Lady Gertrude!' said Corky Beckwith, quite as though they had just encountered one another in the Royal Enclosure at Ascot, rather than behind a curtain in a seedy office building in Aldgate.

She stared at him, one hand on her heart and the other clapped over her mouth, as the two men who had been talking came out of the office and went down the stairs. There came the sound of a door closing; evidently Dauncey and his associate had gone out into the street.

'What are you doing here?' hissed Gertie, once she was sure nobody was coming back. 'I nearly died of fright!'

'I was following you,' replied Corky, with a rare foray into the bare-faced truth.

'What on earth for?'

'Very slow time of year, August. You see, all the politicians take the summer off, and crime rates tend to fall too. One might almost conjecture a connection between the two events, don't you think?' He gave her a view of his teeth and paused to savour his own wit, then went on, 'At any rate, one must get one's news where one can find it—mostly on the social side of things—and you're always good for a few readers. We get a lot of letters about you every time we feature you, as a matter of fact.'

'Really? What do they say?' said Gertie curiously.

'Perhaps that is not a subject for discussion at present,' said Corky delicately. 'One doesn't wish to offend, but I expect you're aware that many of our readers are rather uneducated, and have difficulty in appreciating the nuances to be found in the behaviour of the upper classes.'

Gertie opened her mouth to reply, then thought better of it.

'But why on earth did you follow me here?' she said instead.

'Well, after the hint you graciously vouchsafed on Saturday about yourself and young Pilkington-Soames, I wanted to find out more—whether, in short, the two of you are engaged, so

I took it upon myself to ascertain the truth of the matter on behalf of the readers of the *Herald* and decided to keep you in sight.'

'Do you mean to say you've been following me all morning?'

'Yes, and a most *instructive* morning it's been,' he said. 'Who would have thought one could spend as much as five and a half guineas on a set of cami-knickers and a nightdress? Even if they are Milanese silk with lace trimming.' He leered. 'I must say, peach was a very good choice. The pale yellow would have quite washed you out.'

Gertie directed an outraged glare at him.

'Do you always take this much interest in other people's underthings?'

'Oh, not I, not I. I couldn't be less interested in the intimate raiments of the fairer sex. It's for the readers, naturally. Their appetite for detail is quite insatiable, even where their curiosity demonstrates a certain lack of sophistication. They're mostly interested in knowing the name of the young man on whom you propose to bestow your hand, but little snippets of information about your wardrobe are always very welcome.'

'Readers, my foot!' said Gertie rudely. 'You're nothing but a dirty-minded snoop.'

'Not at all. I refer you to my by-line. Albert Caulfield Beckwith is the name. Sometimes they even spell it right.' He regarded her sideways. 'Incidentally, since we're here and the subject has already been introduced, I don't mind confiding to you that money has been wagered back at the office on the outcome of your hitherto faltering approaches to the married state, and before you go I'd consider it a great favour if you'd be prepared to give me some inside information.'

Gertie stared, open-mouthed.

'Do you mean to say you're running a *book?*'

'Why not? One must have a little harmless amusement, you know.'

'On whether I'll get engaged?'

'Oh, we know you'll get engaged. You do it so often one could almost set a clock by it. It's the name of the next lucky fellow we're looking for. The general consensus at the *Herald* is that you have the young Viscount Delamere in mind—'

'Ugh! No fear of that!' interjected Gertie, appalled.

'—but thanks to my presence at the air show on Saturday, I have knowledge of which my colleagues are unaware, having seen you and Freddy together. Still, in view of the present circumstances, I see that I may have been mistaken, and that your lively eye may in fact have come to rest upon an altogether different personage.'

He gave her a significant look. Gertie was puzzled for a second, then realized to whom he was referring.

'Do you mean Captain Dauncey? Don't be absurd!'

'Then why are you here?'

This was a perfectly reasonable question, to which Gertie had no answer. Fortunately, Corky's mention of the air show gave her an idea.

'Well, you see, I forgot to ask for his autograph on Saturday, and when I happened to see him on Bond Street I decided it might be my last chance. He's awfully famous, isn't he?'

She giggled. It was one of her better giggles, but it did not fool Corky for a second.

'Come now, you don't think I was born yesterday, do you? I know what you're doing. Why, it's quite obvious that Freddy has told you all about our little conversation at the air show, and he's sent you out to do his dirty work for him while he sits idle, waiting to see what you come up with.'

She was about to deny it, when it struck her that discretion was the better part of valour, and that Corky presumably knew nothing of their investigation into the murder of Douglas Westray. It was better that he remain in the dark on this question, so she lowered her eyes and said:

'Yes, it's true: I did say I would try and find out what Captain Dauncey was up to.'

'I knew it! I knew he would try and steal a march on me. Well, you may tell him that I'll have none of it. Dauncey is clearly up to something—I heard it all just as well as you did—but this is *my* story and if Freddy won't share then I won't either—you may tell him that!

'Yes, yes,' said Gertie impatiently, for by now all she wanted to do was get away from him. 'I'll tell him whatever you like.'

She pulled aside the curtain and emerged from the recess. Corky followed her, and they went out into the street together. Gertie looked about. To her relief, there was no sign of Captain Dauncey. She spied a taxi coming towards them on the other side of the road, and before Corky could suggest coming with her, dived into the traffic.

'Are you engaged or not?' he called after her. 'Do tell, won't you? There's a tenner in it for me.'

She ignored him and jumped into the taxi.

'Grosvenor Square,' she said to the driver, then got in and sat back to think over all she had learnt that morning.

Chapter Fifteen

AT THE SAME time as Gertie was following Captain Dauncey into the depths of East London, Freddy was sitting at his desk in the *Clarion's* offices. Although he was physically present at his place of employment, little work was being done. Instead, he was leaning back in his chair, idly firing ink pellets at the ceiling with a ruler, and pondering the riddle of Douglas Westray's death. At present the mystery seemed to consist entirely of loose ends, with nothing to tie them together. The shoes, the pen, the comb, the attempt to run him over, the fact that nobody had heard the gunshot, the question of whether Lois Westray had seen Captain Dauncey on the balcony, Tatty's suspicion that somebody had overheard her conversation with Douglas in the smoking room—all these things and more swirled indistinctly in his head, refusing to form themselves into a pattern. Was it all really as complicated as it seemed? His investigations had led him here and there, but when all was said and done he could not help thinking that the answer must lie with Douglas himself. Who benefited from his death? Nobody, as far as Freddy could tell—or at least, not to the extent of killing him. He had not been rich, and such enemies as he did have—who were not enemies in the strongest sense of the word—had no reason to do away with him. But if it was not a matter of love or hate or money, then why had he been killed? Freddy considered his brief acquaintance with Douglas, who at the time had seemed more of a minor nuisance than anything else, a pebble underfoot which needed sweeping away without much thought. Was that what had happened? Had he been got out of the way for some unknown reason?

Involuntarily Freddy's thoughts went to Captain Dauncey. If any of the people present at the dance that evening might have been said to be careless of life in general, Dauncey was the man. He was certainly careless of his own life, but did that attitude extend to the lives of others? Might he have swept Douglas out of the way if he found him to be an obstacle? Had Douglas known something to Dauncey's disadvantage that made him dangerous? If so, what? But set against the idea of Dauncey as murderer was the incident at the air show, in which he had lost control of his plane. Had someone tampered with the Nugent Nuthatch, as Lord Browncliffe had claimed? If so, was it to prevent the aeroplane from selling well—or had the aim been to put Dauncey out of the way too? Was Dauncey the next intended victim?

And then there was Tom Chetwynd, who had fallen out with Douglas because of his engagement to Tatty. The fact that Douglas had attempted to win her back might, in other circumstances, Freddy supposed, have been a good enough reason for murder, but in this case it did not fit, since Tom seemed strangely unenthusiastic about the marriage, and had quite openly shown that he knew Tatty was still in love with her former fiancé. That did not speak of a crime committed out of rage or jealousy.

Freddy rubbed his chin, puzzled. None of it made sense. Still, there was no use in spending all day brooding in the office. Freddy had a story to write for which he had to go to Kensington, so he abandoned his ink pellets, fetched his hat and went out. He performed his duty for the paper, and after that took a train to Hammersmith, the site of the Westray factory, where Douglas had worked.

The building was a tall, square building situated at the end of a narrow street. Freddy entered and asked the porter whether he might speak to Leslie Penbrigg. Mr. Penbrigg was in the canteen having a bite of lunch, it seemed, but he would most likely be finished soon. At length he appeared, and brightened when he saw his visitor.

'Freddy!' he said. 'This is a surprise. What are you doing here?'

'Hallo, old chap, I thought I'd come and look you up. There's something I want to ask you.'

'Certainly,' said Penbrigg. 'We'll go into my workshop.'

'You mean the centre of operations, where all the clever thinking goes on?'

'Oh, well, I shouldn't say that, exactly,' said Penbrigg, modestly.

He set off along a corridor towards the back of the building. Freddy glanced through the doors as they passed, catching glimpses of people busy at work. Through one door was a huge, high-ceilinged room, and he stopped to look in. It was a large, bright space, with tall windows at one end that let in the light. Set out in neat rows in the middle of the room were trestles, on which were laid wooden structures which Freddy recognized as the beginnings of aeroplane wings. At each trestle stood one or two men in white aprons, bent over their work with drills and planes and glue. Against the wall stood neat stacks of completed wing frames. The floor was covered in wood shavings.

'As you can see, this is where we assemble the wings,' said Penbrigg.

'Are these for fighter planes?' asked Freddy.

'No, these ones are for civilian use,' replied Penbrigg. 'You know, delivering mail and suchlike.'

The next room was equally large and high, with a balcony running around three sides. From the ceiling was suspended part of the fuselage of an aeroplane.

'That's the Ocelot,' said Penbrigg, a touch of pride in his voice. Sir Stanley is hoping we'll receive a big order soon, since it performed so well at the Heston air show.'

'Unlike the Nugent Nuthatch. I suppose Westray will benefit from that?'

'Perhaps,' said Penbrigg. 'It was rather unfortunate for them. I wonder what went wrong.'

'Lord Browncliffe seems to think it was sabotage. He even went so far as to accuse Westray of tampering with the Nugent machine.'

'That's rot, of course!' said Penbrigg indignantly. 'One of their lot made a mistake, that's all, and they tried to save face by accusing us of foul play. It's jolly bad form.'

'Then you don't believe in the sabotage theory? According to Lord Browncliffe one of the fuel lines was cut.'

'If it was, it was nothing to do with Westray. If you ask me, something wasn't fastened tightly enough, and it worked loose.'

'I'll take your word for it. But whatever the cause, presumably it's scuppered the Nuthatch's chances of selling.'

'Not necessarily,' said Penbrigg. 'The Nuthatch is a good machine, and there's another air show at the end of the month down in Shoreham. Perhaps it will do better this time.'

'I take it the Ocelot will be there too. Incidentally, what will happen if you don't get any orders for your plane?'

'Then it won't get made,' said Penbrigg simply.

'It's a pity from your point of view that there won't be a partnership between Westray and Nugent now. If Tatty hadn't thrown Douglas over for Tom Chetwynd then the two companies might have joined forces and perhaps there would have been a promotion in it for you.'

Penbrigg shrugged philosophically.

'There's no use in chewing on these things. Nugent put a lot of money into development, right enough, but there's no saying whether they'd have wanted me. I might have found myself back in a junior position. No, I'm happy enough here.'

He led Freddy out of the building and into a walled yard overgrown with weeds, at the end of which was a large hut of recent construction. He unlocked the door and they went in. This was Penbrigg's workshop, although at first glance it looked more like a junk-room, such was its untidiness. It was darker than the aeroplane workshops, having smaller windows, and Penbrigg switched on an overhead light as they entered, which showed the mess in all its glory. Freddy gazed around him curiously. A long bench stood in the centre of the room, on which were scattered dozens of engine parts and half-built bits of machinery. A single propeller blade was leaning against one wall, and a couple of sections from an aeroplane wing stood against another. The floor was carpeted in wood and metal shavings. Freddy picked his way among the detritus.

'You ought to have this place swept,' he said.

Penbrigg had picked up a piece of paper on which was sketched a rough plan, and was examining it.

'I don't let anyone in here normally,' he said vaguely. 'After someone threw away half the parts of a new type of radial I issued strict instructions that nothing was to be touched.'

He seemed less self-effacing, more at home here. This was Penbrigg's domain, and he was the master of it. He crossed the room and went through a second door, which led into a little office, and came out carrying some more plans, which he spread out on the bench. Freddy went to look at the wing sections.

'Are you still working on wing slots?' he said.

Penbrigg looked up from his plans.

'Oh, yes, there's always more to be learned, and I'm almost certain the design can be improved further. I should like to develop a slot that allows a critical angle of attack of above twenty-five degrees.' He saw Freddy's look of polite incomprehension, and explained: 'It means the aeroplanes of the future will be able to fly at very low speeds and still remain in the air.'

'I see.' Freddy turned to the workbench and saw a vice, which was clamped round a half-formed cylinder of metal, in which a number of holes had been drilled. 'What's this?'

'An engine muffler,' said Penbrigg. 'That's an early version. I have a new one that's fully functional now, but that's locked away until we can get it patented.'

Freddy supposed he had learned his lesson from the disaster of the wing slot patent, and did not wish to leave anything to chance. He cast his eye across the bench and picked up a small device with a small, hook-like protuberance at one end, on which was stamped the name 'Westray' in tiny letters. 'Sparking plug?' he said.

'That's right. It's quite an ordinary one, but with a new design of electrode. The first few we made had a flaw in the metal, and the electrode kept snapping off, but I think we've got it right now.' He took the plug and regarded it critically, then laid it to one side. 'So, how can I help you?'

'As a matter of fact, I'm still looking into this affair of poor old Douglas, and whether it really was suicide,' said Freddy.

Penbrigg looked surprised.

'You don't think he killed himself?'

'Well I can't prove anything to the contrary, and to be perfectly honest I was coming to the conclusion that it was all a mare's nest—that is, until somebody tried to run me over deliberately.'

'Not really? Run you over? How?'

Freddy related the events of Saturday night and indicated the scrape on his left cheek.

'So that's where you got it,' said Penbrigg. 'I assumed you'd been fighting.'

Freddy suppressed an exasperated sigh.

'No, it wasn't a fight—unless you call being smacked in the face by Fleet Street fighting. Anyway, as you can imagine, I take exception to having cars driven at me, and I'd rather like to know who did it and why.'

'But what makes you think it had anything to do with Douglas's death? Don't you reporter fellows always have criminals out for your blood?'

'Not as a rule. No, I'm almost sure someone heard me asking around and decided to put me out of the way—a mistake on his part, as all he's done is to make me even more curious than I was before.'

'Yes, I can see why. Very well, what do you want of me?'

'I'd like to see Douglas's office, if I may, and you're the only person who can show it to me apart from Sir Stanley, but I didn't want to agitate him.'

'He's away in Cowes with Alida and Lady Westray until Thursday, anyway,' said Penbrigg. 'Why do you want to see Douglas's office?'

'I gather someone broke into his drawer after his death, and I'd like to take a look. I don't suppose it will help much, but one must explore all avenues.'

'I suppose so. All right, I'll take you in there. It's in the main building.'

They left the workshop and Penbrigg locked it carefully, then led Freddy into the factory and up some stairs to the first floor, to the room which had been Douglas Westray's office. It was much plainer than Freddy had expected; in fact, there was not much to it at all—just a desk, a chair and one or two cupboards. Under the window stood a drawing-board, on which some blueprints were laid out.

'Not exactly luxurious, is it?' said Freddy.

'I don't think Douglas was especially interested in that sort of thing,' said Penbrigg.

Freddy went across to the desk, which was plain, like the rest of the room, and had only two drawers, of which the top one had been forced open. Inside were a few pencils, a pair of scissors and some bits of paper. Freddy flicked through the papers.

'Nothing of interest,' he said. 'When did the break-in happen, exactly?'

'Nobody's quite sure. Douglas didn't come into the factory that week, so it might have happened at any time—a few days before he died, even.'

'And no-one knows what was taken, if anything?'

Penbrigg shook his head.

Freddy gave it up. He did not know what he had been hoping to find, but whatever it was, it was certainly not here. He thanked Penbrigg and prepared to leave.

'By the way,' he said. 'Any further forward with Alida?'

Penbrigg flushed.

'N—no,' he said.

'I'd just ask her if I were you, old chap, before someone else comes in and swipes her from under your nose. Time and women wait for no man.'

'She wouldn't look at me. I can't ask her anything until I've made a name for myself. She'll say no.'

'Not if she likes you. Oh well, I suppose you know best. And now I'd better get back to the office. Cheerio!'

He started off towards the stairs, leaving Leslie Penbrigg staring after him.

That evening Gertie telephoned Freddy, bursting to tell him about her adventure of that day. Freddy listened, preparing to be exasperated, but then grew interested as she told him of the office in Aldgate and the conversation she had overheard.

'So he is up to something!' he exclaimed. 'And whatever it is, he's being well paid for it. Who was the other man? Did you see him at all?'

'No. I had to hide quickly when they came out, and didn't get a chance to look at him. He spoke English but he was certainly foreign.'

'Did you recognize the accent?'

'No. It wasn't one I've heard before—not French or German, or anything like that. And he had a gun! I heard him threatening Dauncey with it.'

'My word!' said Freddy. 'Dauncey taking money from mysterious foreigners in exchange for his honour. I wonder what he's doing. This could be a huge story, if only I can find out what he's been up to.'

'Well, you'd better hurry,' said Gertie. 'Your pal Corky is on his trail too.'

'Corky? How do you know?'

'Because he followed me and Captain Dauncey all the way to Aldgate and hid behind a curtain watching me while I was listening at the door.'

'What?'

'Oh, yes. He gave me the most awful fright. I don't know how he got there without my spotting him.'

'I imagine he slithered up through the sewers. He's had plenty of practice.'

'Would you believe they've got a book running at the *Herald* as to who I'll get engaged to next?' she said in disgust.

'Surely not!' said Freddy, doing his best to sound shocked, although in truth a similar scheme was in place at the *Clarion*. 'Who's favourite, by the way?' he could not help asking casually.

'Bill Delamere, if you'll believe it!'

'Delamere? Interesting. Why do they think that? Anything happening there?' said Freddy, poised to take a note and recalculating odds in his head.

'No! And why are you so interested, anyway? Listen, forget that, we need to find out what Dauncey is doing.'

'What did you say was the name of the man the foreigner mentioned?'

'Let me think. What was it, now? Something to do with fish.'

'Mr. Rodd? Mr. Guppy? Mr. Haddock? Mr. Trout?'

'No, silly. Something foreign.' She thought. 'Salmanov! That was it!'

'And what exactly did the other man say about him?'

'Nothing in particular. Dauncey just said he didn't want to do whatever it was any more, and the foreign man said, "We shall see what Mr. Salmanov says." Then Dauncey went into a miff.'

'And what was the name of the company?'

'Stamboul International Export Co.'

'I've never heard of it. I shall have to see what I can find out.'

'Very well,' said Gertie. 'And in the meantime, what shall I do? I've a taste for investigation now, and I feel we're hot on the scent.'

'I don't think there's much else you can do about Dauncey for the moment. If there are chaps waving guns about then you're better off staying out of it.'

'But I want to do something. Are you going to the Chetwynds' garden-party on Saturday?'

'I don't remember whether I've had an invitation, but if I haven't I shall crash the place in my capacity as press.'

'Good. We can do some more investigating there. I'm almost sure we're just about to discover something really important.'

'I hope so,' said Freddy.

The next day, Freddy left the *Clarion's* offices at lunch-time and went to a stately-looking building on Gresham Street, where his father was normally to be found on weekdays. Herbert Pilkington-Soames was large and bald with a red face and a moustache, and was as unlike Freddy as it was possible to be. Although he was very fond of his wife and son, he much preferred a quiet life—something which was not to be had when in their company—and so he took every opportunity to escape to the City, where he passed his days reasonably peacefully as chairman of a large banking institution. When Freddy announced himself unexpectedly in the lobby of the building, a functionary gave him a glance of alarm and telephoned up to ask if Mr. Pilkington-Soames might be available to see his son. After some little delay, Freddy was told he might go up. When he went into his father's office he found Herbert sitting behind his desk, dictating a letter collectedly to a cool young woman with very fair hair. She excused herself as soon as Freddy arrived, but Herbert's eyes lingered on her as she left.

'Hallo, Freddy, what are you doing here?' he said jovially. 'Oughtn't you to be at work, rooting out scandals?'

'I am—in a manner of speaking, at least. I want to ask you a question.'

'What?' said Herbert. An expression of panic passed briefly across his face.

'It's about a chap called Salmanov.'

'Oh.' Herbert's face cleared. 'Salmanov, yes. I've heard of the fellow. What do you want to know?' He glanced at his watch. 'Let's go for lunch, and we can talk about it then.'

Freddy needed no persuading, and they went to a place his father frequented regularly.

'So, what do you know about this man Salmanov?' prompted Freddy, once they had been seated in a comfortable corner.

'That depends on whether it's the same fellow,' said Herbert. 'I assume we're talking about Anatoli Salmanov.'

'I don't know, exactly. Who is Anatoli Salmanov?'

'He's a well-known figure in the world of international munitions and engineering. He's what they call a "fixer", and he's behind some of the biggest procurement agreements of recent times between governments, but he's not above sabotaging the competition in order to win a sale, and his name has been linked to a number of scandals, including the collapse of a huge copper mining company in the Dutch East Indies a few years ago.'

'Not the Celebes scandal?' said Freddy in surprise. 'Is that the same chap? The one who's always mentioned in hushed terms on the foreign news pages? I remember the copper mine affair—he sold it to a Dutch company after producing fraudulent evidence that there was plenty of ore left, but after the deeds had been signed it was discovered that the thing had been completely worked out. And then he was mixed up in some sabotage story in Spain—something to do with a new gunboat, wasn't it?'

'That's the fellow,' agreed Herbert. 'Of course, he denies absolutely having had anything to do with any of these things, and claims that he merely acted as agent in both cases. But there's no smoke without fire, as they say, and there are several other instances I could name but won't, in which underhanded dealing has been suspected in connection with his name—mostly to do with the sale of faulty parts. So, what's the story? Anything I ought to know about?'

'I'm not sure. What's he doing now?'

'He went to earth for a while after the Spanish fiasco, but I rather think he's working for one of Rawson Welbeck's subsidiaries in Turkey or Greece, or somewhere like that.'

'Rawson Welbeck? That's interesting,' said Freddy thoughtfully. Rawson Welbeck was an international conglomerate, much bigger than Westray Enterprises and Nugent Corporation, with interests in many countries. It was known for its ruthless business dealings, and had on many occasions been caught up in lawsuits with other companies, so it was hardly surprising to learn that such a man as Salmanov was working for them now. Rawson Welbeck had exhibited two of its own fighter planes at the air show alongside the Nugent Nuthatch and the Westray Ocelot, and stood to benefit from the bad performance of the Nuthatch at the air display in the form of possible government contracts. If Captain Dauncey was taking money from Anatoli Salmanov, then it was almost certain that he had been acting to the disadvantage of Nugent Corporation. Had he, then, sabotaged the Nugent Nuthatch himself? What a risk he had taken, if that were so! Freddy could hardly believe it. Why, Dauncey might easily have died had he not managed to maintain control of the aircraft, and might easily have killed many other people in addition to himself. It was a testament to his expertise as a pilot that he had succeeded in landing it safely. It was starting to look as though Corky had been right, and that Captain Dauncey was not the man the nation believed him to be. But what, if anything, was the connection with Douglas Westray? Freddy felt he was close to finding out, but could not help thinking that a vital piece of the puzzle was still missing—and until he found that, the mystery would remain unsolved.

Chapter Sixteen

THE CHETWYNDS' SUMMER garden party had, in recent times, become quite a fixture in the social calendar. The first one had been held some five years ago, and had proved such a success that there had seemed no reason not to repeat it. So it was that on a convenient Saturday every August, the great and the good—and many others who could be classified as neither—flocked to River View Hall just outside Henley to enjoy the generous hospitality of Sir Thomas and Lady Bryce Chetwynd, eat their food, and drink their wine. As its name suggested, the house was set atop a gentle rise, from where its large lawns sloped down to the Thames at a point where the river curved in a particularly picturesque manner. The morning had threatened rain, but the danger had passed, and now the sky was blue and serene, with barely a wisp of cloud to be seen. When Freddy arrived he found the festivities in full swing, with at least a hundred people scattered around the lawn in groups, drinking champagne, talking and laughing. Freddy looked about him and soon spotted Lord and Lady

Browncliffe talking to Alida Westray. Gertie was in attendance with her parents, the Earl and Countess of Strathmerrick, and was wearing her most innocent expression as she talked to Sir Thomas.

'Hallo, Freddy,' said a voice beside him, and he turned to see Lois Westray, looking fresh and pretty, with a glass of champagne in her hand.

'Lois,' said Freddy. 'How was Cowes?'

'Oh, the usual,' she replied. 'There were lots of boats and one couldn't see who was winning. The weather was decent, so I suppose one ought to be thankful for that at least, but I much prefer London.'

They stood for a few moments, remarking on the weather and the success of the party, while Freddy deliberated inwardly. It had been agreed that Gertie should be the one to speak to Lois, but she had just button-holed Tom Chetwynd and was talking to him, and it was a pity to let this opportunity slip through his fingers. He made up his mind and decided to risk a direct accusation.

'Lois,' he said, 'why did you lie about being on the balcony with Captain Dauncey on the night Douglas died?'

She blinked at the sudden change of subject.

'I saw you come down the stairs just before him,' he explained. 'If you weren't there together, then you must have seen him—unless of course you didn't see him because he wasn't there.'

He was almost sure this was not the case, but he wanted to be certain. Lois seemed to sag. She glanced around, then turned a bleak look on him.

'I hoped you hadn't seen me,' she said. 'But I really ought to stop trying to cover it up, as it's done nobody any good at all. If you only knew the guilt I've been suffering since Doug died, at the thought that it might have been all my fault!'

'Why do you think it was your fault?'

She glanced around again.

'I'd rather not be overheard,' she said.

They walked down to the bottom of the garden and sat on a bench overlooking the river, and Lois stared into her glass and began to talk.

'Frank and I were married for a short while,' she said. 'It was just before the war, and I was very young. I was in the States, trying to make a name for myself in the theatre as an actress, and he was over there racing cars—you know he won the Vanderbilt Cup two years running? We met and married far too quickly. It was absurd, really. I loved him but he was quite impossible to live with, and so we divorced. Then I came back to England and married David and gave up trying to be an actress, and we were very happy for many years until he died. I didn't see Frank at all during that time, but when I married Stanley we began running across one another frequently because of Frank's work for the Nugent Corporation. I kept quiet about knowing Frank already because Stanley didn't like him and he's rather stuffy about divorce, and I'd never mentioned it because I thought of it as a mistake I'd made when I was too young to know better. But from the beginning Frank behaved as though we'd never been apart, even though he knew I didn't want to be reminded about it. He just laughed when I told him not to come and see me, and kept on doing it anyway. Then one day he came and said he was flat broke and could I sub him? He was always terrible with money—that was one of the things we rowed about from the start after our marriage. He said he couldn't make his way in the Air Force any more because they'd more or less told him to leave after some incident or other, and so he had to find other ways of supporting himself.'

'They threw him out?'

'Not exactly. I think it was by mutual agreement. It would have looked bad if they'd discharged him for misconduct when he was such a national hero and had won so many medals, but they didn't want to keep him on, and so he departed quietly.'

'What did he do?'

'According to *him*, nothing. He said there'd been some unfortunate accident here in England in which two of his fellow-officers died, and he'd been unjustly accused of causing their deaths by being drunk on duty. He denied it, of course. Still, the fact is he left the flying corps quietly and had trouble getting steady employment afterwards. That's why he came to me. I didn't have anything to give him and told him so, but he wouldn't leave me alone.' She sighed. 'He always knew how to talk me round, and I thought it would stop him pestering me about the money, so I let him do it.'

'Let him do what?'

She turned her head away.

'I let him into Doug's office at the factory while Doug was away in Deauville,' she said. 'He said he'd heard there was some new wing design in the offing, and he wanted to see the plans. It was just curiosity, he said. He wanted to see how far ahead of Nugent Westray had got, since the Woodville Prize was coming up.' She turned back to gaze at Freddy miserably. 'It oughtn't to have mattered—it wouldn't have mattered, except—'

'Except that Douglas had forgotten to register the patent on behalf of Westray,' said Freddy.

She nodded.

'I would never have done it if I'd known. I don't suppose you can imagine how dreadful I felt when Douglas came back and it turned out that Nugent had somehow registered an almost identical patent before him. There were all sorts of rows for weeks, and then Nugent won the Woodville Prize using the wing slots invented by Westray, and Stanley accused Douglas of passing on the design to Tatty, and there was a falling-out. And I, like the terrible coward I am, kept quiet all the way through,' she finished bitterly. 'It was all my fault. If I hadn't let Frank see the plans then Douglas would have remembered to register the patent as soon as he got back from Deauville and Westray would have won the Woodville Prize.'

Freddy just then remembered a remark Douglas had made on the night of the dance.

'Did Douglas know you were the one to blame?' he said.

She nodded.

'Yes. I'm not sure how he found out. I think Frank probably let it slip when he'd been drinking. The two of them were friends of a sort. I'd told Frank not to mention that we'd once been married, but I was always frightened he'd say something.'

'And did he?'

'Not as far as I know, but he must have told Douglas about what I'd done, because Doug came and confronted me about it. Of course I had to admit to it then, and explained why I'd done it, and that I didn't want Stanley to know about my past.' She blinked, as though trying to hold back tears. 'He was a good boy, you know, Freddy. He was tremendously kind at heart. I was all set to go and confess to Stanley, but then Doug gave me that mournful, hang-dog look of his and said he was already in trouble for forgetting to register the patent, so he might as well be hung for a sheep as a lamb, and there was no need for his father to know. He didn't admit to having done it, exactly, but he let Stanley think he had. The trouble was Stanley wouldn't let it go, although I tried my best to smooth things over between them, knowing what Doug had done for me. But it was no use. And then it all ended between him and Tatty, and Tatty got engaged to Tom Chetwynd, and somehow Doug thought it was a good idea to get engaged to Gertie and then *that* ended too—' she stopped, and sighed again.

'And then Douglas was found dead and you thought you'd driven him to it.'

'Yes,' she said in a small voice. 'You can't imagine how I've been turning the whole thing over and over in my mind ever since he died, and wishing more than anything that I'd simply confessed to Stanley about Frank as soon as I married him. After all, it's nothing so very shameful these days, and I was very young. And now I have to face the probability that I caused my step-son's suicide because of my own cowardice.'

'I'm not certain you did, old thing,' said Freddy.

'What do you mean?'

'I've been doing a little investigating since we met that day in Harrods, and I'm rather coming around to Tatty's way of seeing things.'

She looked up.

'You mean it *was* murder after all?'

'Yes, I think it was.'

'But how? How is that possible? I thought Tatty was just feeling as guilty about him as I did, and that's why she was so insistent on its being murder. But I never for a moment thought it was actually true. If someone killed him then how did they get into a locked room?'

'How they got *into* it is easy enough—it's how they got *out* of it that's the difficult part. But I have a little idea about that.'

'Is it terrible of me to hope against hope that it *was* murder?' she said. 'I suppose it is. But I can't help my own selfishness—if I thought for a minute that Douglas's death wasn't my fault I should be so relieved!'

'Then tell me the truth: did you see Dauncey up on the balcony that night?'

'Yes, I did. He followed me up there and started bothering me. He wanted me to let him into Doug's office again—or better still, Leslie Penbrigg's workshop. I told him in no uncertain terms that I didn't have a key to Leslie's room, and I shouldn't let him in even if I did, and the same went for Doug's office. He wasn't at all pleased at that—he started hinting that he'd tell Stanley about what I'd done, and that I ought to help him whenever he asked me, because of what we'd once been to each other. That made me angry. I said there was no use in his threatening me, since I'd been thinking of confessing to

Stanley anyway, and if he really wanted the world to know that he was a thief, and that Nugent had won the Woodville Prize on the strength of a stolen design, then he was welcome to put an advertisement in the *Times* if he liked. That shut him up.'

'Were you on the balcony with him all the time? I mean, he didn't jimmy open the window while your back was turned and disappear for a minute or two?'

'No, of course not. We talked, then I came down the stairs, and he came down shortly afterwards.'

'Yes, it was too soon afterwards for him to have done it that way. Does Lord Browncliffe know what Dauncey's been up to, by the way? Does he know the wing slot design was stolen?'

'I don't believe he does. I don't think he knows half of what goes on in his own company, as a matter of fact. He likes to wave his hand and have things done for him, but doesn't want to bother about the details. If one of his employees showed him a new invention that was likely to win a prize it wouldn't occur to him to look into it too closely.'

'I see,' said Freddy. He thought for a moment. 'Tatty told me that Dauncey and Douglas were friends at one time, but then fell out around the time the Woodville Prize was awarded. I rather wonder whether you mightn't have been the reason.'

'Perhaps I was. Doug wasn't the secretive sort. I think having to keep quiet about me sat badly with him, and I shouldn't be at all surprised if he'd decided to go and vent his feelings to Frank's face.'

'If he did, don't you think that's a good enough reason for murder?'

Lois stared.

'You mean Frank?'

'Yes. If he thought he was about to be exposed, don't you think he might have decided to put Douglas out of the way?'

She hesitated.

'I don't know. This all happened last year. If Frank was going to do it, wouldn't he have done it at the time?'

'He might. Or he might have assumed he was safe until the night of the dance, when Douglas had too much to drink and started causing trouble. What if Douglas threatened Dauncey that evening? He was drunk enough to have announced what he knew to the world, and Dauncey certainly wouldn't have wanted that. What if he decided to put Douglas out of the way to ensure his silence once and for all?'

'Why, I—' she stopped. 'I don't know,' she said at last.

'Nor do I,' said Freddy. 'That's the trouble.'

Chapter Seventeen

FOR THE NEXT hour, Freddy did his social duty. He paid his compliments to the hostess, flattered Sir Thomas, and passed the time with Tom and Tatty, who were wandering around the garden together wearing fixed smiles that were not altogether convincing. After that he mingled with the other guests, discussing politics, flirting, or making fatuous jokes as required. Then, finding himself momentarily bereft of company, he took a stroll down to a little cluster of bushes at the bottom of the garden, where he found Leslie Penbrigg and Alida Westray standing together in halting conversation. Penbrigg was pink in the face, and his expression reminded Freddy of nothing so much as a stupefied sheep, while Alida, also blushing a little, seemed to be doing her best to encourage him. It was hardly Romeo and Juliet, but Freddy considered it a step forward that Penbrigg had made it as far as talking to her, and decided to leave them alone. At length he was accosted by Gertie.

'What a bore!' she said. 'I've been talking to people for hours and nobody has anything entertaining to say. Tell me something interesting, but I warn you, if you so much as mention the weather I shall scream. At last count I've agreed forty-three times that it's a beautiful day.'

'Oh, you want something interesting, do you? Very well, what about this: Lois Westray used to be married to Captain Dauncey and passed on the Westray wing slot design to him.'

If he had been hoping to create a sensation with this piece of news he was not disappointed. Gertie gaped at him, dumbfounded.

'No!' she said, once she had found her voice. 'Come on then, my boy, dish it up!'

Freddy told her what Lois had said and she listened, open-mouthed.

'Well!' she said at last. 'There's another motive for murder if ever there was one! Doug must have threatened to expose Dauncey for stealing the wing slot plans.'

'It's certainly possible,' agreed Freddy, 'although we still have no evidence of any of this. At any rate, it's something we didn't know before. All we have to do now is to work out how—or if—it fits into the question.'

'Of course it fits in. Give me a cigarette, will you? Not here—Mother doesn't approve. Let's go somewhere and think it out in private.'

They left the garden by the path along the river, and walked along the bank a little way together, until they reached a secluded, shady spot close to a wooden landing-stage. Gertie threw herself down under a tree.

'Let's stay here and look at the clues one by one,' she said.

But the day and the scenery were too pleasant to be thinking about murder; moreover, the weather and the champagne were having a soporific effect, so instead they sat and smoked in a companionable silence. Gertie leaned back against the tree trunk and closed her eyes, while Freddy idly watched a kingfisher which was perched on a low-hanging branch by the water, preparing to dive. After a few minutes he saw coming along the path towards them a girl, walking slowly, her eyes turned down towards the ground. Freddy's attention was caught by her, firstly because even from that distance it was clear that she was very pretty; and secondly because she was wearing a coat which was far too heavy for the weather. She had not seen them, and as he watched he saw that she was behaving somewhat oddly. Her eyes scanned the path and the river bank, and occasionally she would stoop and pick up a stone. By the landing-stage was a patch of gravel, and she stopped here and picked up several large stones and put them in her pocket. Freddy was struck by her fixed gaze and her sense of purpose.

'Queer,' he said to himself.

'If there were any boats around here one might go out on the river,' remarked Gertie, without opening her eyes.

Freddy was still watching the girl. She had by now filled her pockets with stones and was making her way along to the little landing-stage. She stepped onto it and walked along to the end. At last Freddy understood what she was about to do, and stood up.

'Hi!' he shouted, but it was too late, for the girl had jumped off the landing-stage without a second's hesitation. Gertie opened her eyes at his shout, and was just in time to see the girl disappear under the water. She gasped. Freddy saw there was no time to lose and sprang into action. He dashed down to the edge of the river, closely followed by Gertie, threw off his jacket and shoes, and hurled himself off the jetty after the girl. It was not the most elegant dive, and the freezing water was a shock after the heat of the day, but he did not stop to think about those things, and instead swam two strong strokes, took a deep breath and went under, feeling the water soak heavily into his shirt and trousers, impeding his movement. It was difficult to see anything because of the mud which had been churned up by the disturbance, but he dived towards where he thought the girl might be, and as luck would have it, felt his hand knock against something soft almost immediately. He clutched at her arm, and she struggled a little, but he did not hesitate. The overcoat with the stones in was weighing her down, but there was no time to try and pull it off her, so he took hold of her under the arms and kicked upwards as hard as he could. It seemed to take an age, and his lungs felt as though they were about to explode, but just as he thought he would have to take a breath they burst free of the surface. Freddy took in a huge gasp of air, then began to drag her towards the jetty with difficulty, for she was a dead weight in his arms. Gertie was leaning over the edge of the landing-stage, holding her hands out to help, and between them they managed to get the girl out of the water and carry her across to the grass. She was coughing and gasping, but thanks to Freddy's quick thinking she had not been under the water more than half a minute, and it was soon evident that she had come to no great harm, so Gertie ran off to get some blankets. At last the coughing subsided, and the girl sat quietly, getting her breath back. Her dark hair was plastered to her head, and her large brown eyes were glaring at Freddy with no sign of gratitude.

'You beast!' she said furiously, as soon as she could speak. 'I wanted to do it in peace and quiet while everybody was at the party, and now the story will be all over the place!'

'Well, I was hardly going to stand there and watch you drown, was I?' said Freddy. 'Are you all right?'

'Of course I'm not all right,' she snapped. 'Why do you think I threw myself in?'

She burst into tears, and he regarded her awkwardly. Suicidal women did not figure largely in his experience, and he had no idea what to do next, except make sure she did not try to jump in the river again. He retreated a few feet away and tried to wring out his clothes as best he could, although he feared they were ruined, then spread out his arms to allow the sun to dry him. Eventually, Gertie returned with Tom and Tatty, much to his relief. Tatty was carrying a picnic blanket. The girl's sobs had subsided, but as the others approached they started up again.

'Now look what you've done!' she said.

Tom Chetwynd stopped dead and stared at her, aghast.

'Irene!' he exclaimed. 'What the devil—?'

Tatty gave an exclamation at the sight of the girl, and hurried forward.

'We must get you indoors,' she said. 'We'll take you to the house.'

'No!' said the girl in horror. 'Take me home if you must, but please don't parade me in front of the party—I couldn't bear it! My house is just nearby. Please take me there instead.'

'Well, then, all right,' said Tatty. 'But you'll catch your death of cold in those clothes. Here, let's take the coat off you. This blanket will keep you warm.'

She and Gertie removed her coat between them.

'Oh!' they said together.

'We'll get you a doctor,' said Gertie.

'You must get to bed and rest with your feet up,' said Tatty.

'Perhaps a hot bath first,' said Gertie.

The girl protested, but Tatty wrapped her in the blanket and led her off, followed by Tom, who was white in the face and seemed to have been struck speechless.

Freddy, still feeling damp and uncomfortable, put on his shoes then picked up his jacket and followed with Gertie.

'I wonder what brought that on,' he murmured as they walked.

'I should have thought it was obvious,' replied Gertie, then at his blank look, hissed, 'She's in the family way, you idiot! Didn't you notice? And no wedding-ring.'

'Good Lord!' said Freddy, who had noticed the lack of a wedding-ring, but nothing else.

'Poor thing,' went on Gertie. 'It's too bad. I should like to give whoever's responsible a piece of my mind.'

They soon reached the little cottage where the girl lived, and she led the way in. She had stopped protesting and seemed quite resigned, defeated, even.

'Is there anybody we can call? Who lives here with you?' said Gertie.

'I live here alone,' she said.

'What about your parents?'

'They're dead. Listen, it's awfully kind of you but I'm quite well now, so there's no need for you to stay.'

'But we can't leave you alone until we're sure there's someone to look after you,' said Gertie.

'There must be someone we can call,' said Tatty, with a meaningful glance at the girl's middle region.

The girl flushed and turned her face away.

'No,' she said. 'There's no-one.'

'That's not true,' said Tom suddenly, and they all turned to look at him. His jaw was set firmly, and he looked as though he had made up his mind to something. The girl called Irene had been studiously ignoring him, but now she raised her eyes to his. Tom took a step forward.

'Why did you do it, Irene?' he said. 'There was no need for it. I'd have thought of something sooner or later.'

She gave a short laugh.

'Sooner or later? How much later? After the wedding? It would have been too late then. No, this way was better for everyone.'

Tatty was staring from one to the other of them, her face reflecting a dawning realization. Now she straightened up and addressed herself to her intended.

'I think you'd better tell me what's going on, Tom,' she said.

Chapter Eighteen

A DOCTOR HAD BEEN called and was seeing to Irene, while Tatty and Gertie hovered about, trying to be helpful. They had told him that Irene had fallen into the river accidentally, since it seemed harsh on the poor girl that an attempted suicide should be added to her list of sins. Meanwhile, Freddy and Tom sat outside the cottage, smoking, and in Freddy's case, drying off in the sunshine. After holding in his secret for so long, Tom seemed only too relieved to get the story off his chest. Irene Parker was a teacher at a local infant school, it appeared. Her mother had also been a teacher, but her father was old Silas Parker, who had had a butcher's shop in Reading.

'I knew her when we were kids,' said Tom. 'Then I went abroad for a couple of years, and when I got back I bumped into her and fell like a stone—and I thought she fell for me, too. Well, you've seen her, Freddy. She's sweet and pretty and clever—much cleverer than I am. I never did have much in the way of brains, you know, but she'd read a lot, and knew all sorts of things. And she was sensible, too, and kind. Any man would be lucky to have her. But Father didn't agree. He knew what was going on, but I suppose he thought it wasn't a serious thing—he would never have dreamt of stooping to marry a tradesman's daughter himself, you see. But when I came to him and said we were engaged he went off the deep end and said he wouldn't hear of it, and that I couldn't go marrying someone of that class. He said some things about her that were pretty stiff, and we had a row over it, and he said he would disinherit me if I went ahead with it. I shouldn't have cared in the slightest—I was still determined to do it, and told Irene so, but she didn't agree and was all for nobly letting me go. It turned out Father had visited her to say that she ought not to hold me to the engagement because it really wasn't quite the thing, and that she would be acting to my disadvantage if she insisted on marrying me. Somehow he convinced her that he was right, and she broke it off. She said she was doing it for my sake, but I couldn't see it that way. I couldn't budge her, so we had a row and parted on bad terms. I was furious with her, so when Tatty came along I let myself be swept into the engagement. I told myself that would show her. I don't know what I thought it would show her, but I was so angry I wasn't thinking straight.

'I'd wanted to play the whole thing down and not make a big fanfare, but Mother and Father and the Browncliffes would insist on announcing the engagement to the world, and holding dinners and balls, and parading us about in public. I don't think Tatty wanted any of that stuff either. She's a good sort, but it was obvious she was regretting Doug. At any rate, we both went along with it, as we didn't seem to have much choice.

'Then on the afternoon of that damned ball I had a letter from Irene that she'd written in an awful hurry. She'd just found out—you know—and had been thrown into a panic, and wrote to me on the spur of the moment, because there was nobody else she could tell. I don't mind saying it gave me a dreadful shock. I don't know how I managed to get through the evening—I felt sick, and was sure people must have guessed what had happened, and were looking at me and whispering behind their hands. All I could think was that I'd agreed to marry Tatty in front of the whole world, and it would cause a fearful scandal if I broke it off, and Lord Browncliffe might even convince her to sue me for breach of promise. I seemed to have got myself into an impossible hole and I had no idea how to get out of it. After the ball I came down to see Irene, and she said she'd read about it all in the papers and wished she hadn't written the letter, as it was all too late now that everybody was talking about my engagement to Tatty, and I couldn't possibly back out, as it would be too humiliating if everyone knew the truth. And my father would certainly disinherit me, and what were we to do?

'I'm ashamed to say I had no idea what to do either. She was right that it would have caused a lot of talk. I wanted to do the right thing but I'm afraid I dithered and couldn't face up to it, and hoped it would go away. I couldn't see how to break it off with Tatty without a fuss, but I thought she might break it off with me once she came to herself and realized that we weren't exactly suited. She didn't, though, and time went on, and I still hadn't plucked up the courage to act. Of course I had no intention of leaving Irene penniless, but I saw I was about to find myself in the despicable position of being married to one woman while secretly supporting another woman and her—our child. However, it seems Irene had no intention of waiting for me to do the decent thing, and had made other plans in the meantime. So here you see me. You don't need to tell me what a brute I am. I've betrayed one woman and driven another to suicide. Not a bad day's work, eh?' He laughed bitterly.

'I'm sorry, old thing,' said Freddy.

Tom shrugged and stared moodily at his cigarette. Freddy remembered something.

'Douglas knew, didn't he?' he said.

'Yes. He came to see me on the night of the ball. He'd been cool with me ever since I'd got engaged to Tatty, which was understandable. She'd ended things with him weeks before, and latched onto me just to annoy him, I should say—although she'll deny it. Doug was polite enough, but it was obvious he was hurt, and he was stiff and distant the next few times we met. I felt bad about it, so in the end I scrawled him a note saying I hadn't meant to offend him, and I'd be awfully glad to be friends again, which was true, but drat the fellow if he didn't turn up at my flat just as I was reading Irene's letter. He always did have a rotten sense of timing. I let him in and said something—I don't remember what, because my head was spinning. He didn't notice anything was wrong at first, just said he'd got my note and was glad, because he'd been about to do the same thing. I wasn't thinking straight, but I gathered he was prepared to let bygones be bygones, and wanted to talk to me about something. He started to tell me what it was, but then he must have seen I wasn't myself and asked if

I was all right. If I hadn't been in such a stew I shouldn't have said a word, but I blurted it all out to him there and then, and straightaway kicked myself for a fool, because of course his first thought was about what I'd done to Tatty. He told me in no uncertain words what he thought of me, and said if I didn't confess to Tatty then he would tell her. I could see he meant what he said, so I promised I'd talk to her, but said it would be much better if it came from me rather than him. He agreed to keep quiet about it that evening, at least, then went away. Then that night—well, you know what happened. He killed himself, and I felt dreadful about it, but not dreadful enough to come clean to Tatty.'

'What had he come to talk to you about? Can you remember?'

'What? Oh, I don't know—I suppose I was too wrapped up in myself to take much notice. He was bothered about something—someone had got away with murder, he said. I imagine somebody had cheated him at cards or something of the kind. But as soon as I told him about Irene he forgot about whatever it was, and laid into me instead.'

'I see,' said Freddy thoughtfully.

'You may come in now,' said Gertie just then from the door. 'We're all finished.'

They found the doctor in Irene's tiny parlour, just preparing to leave, while Irene herself was reclining on a sofa. She had changed into dry clothes and a blanket was tucked around her.

'But I've told you, I'm quite all right,' she was saying exasperatedly.

'Listen to the doctor,' said Tatty. 'You must get some rest. I'll bet you haven't slept much lately, have you?'

'Not much,' she admitted.

'Well, that won't do you or the baby any good,' said the doctor briskly. 'Now, if the man who did this was any sort of gentleman, he'd be here to look after you. Where is he, by the way? Run off in a fright, I expect.'

'He's not here, but he'll be back soon. They're getting married,' said Tatty firmly, to everyone's surprise.

'Hmph! Better late than never, I suppose, but it never does to put the cart before the horse, young lady.'

He gave Irene a stern look and went off, leaving the five of them awkwardly avoiding one another's eyes. There was a silence.

'Tatty—' began Tom at last.

Tatty drew herself up and glared at him.

'Now, just you listen to me, Tom Chetwynd,' she said severely. 'I don't know how you thought you were going to dig yourself out of this mess, but if you'd only stood up to your father then you'd never have got into it in the first place. Irene has told me everything, and it seems to me the whole thing has got completely out of hand. If you think I'm going to marry you when this poor girl has such a claim over you, then you're quite mistaken, and if you've any sense of honour at all you'll whisk her off to a registry office at once, so she can show her face in public again.'

'Yes, yes, of course I will. Irene, you'll forgive me, won't you? My head was so muddled I couldn't think straight, but I'll stand by you. I won't leave you alone any more.'

She started crying, and he threw himself down on the floor next to the sofa and took her hand.

'Don't be like that, darling—it'll be all right, you'll see.'

'But what about your father?'

'Tatty's right. I never ought to have listened to him in the first place. This time I'll do the right thing by you, I promise, and never mind him. I shall get a licence on Monday and we'll be married as soon as they'll let us. He may come to the wedding if he likes, but if he doesn't, then we won't miss him.' He regarded her with a doubtful expression. 'You—you do *want* to get married, don't you?'

She nodded fervently through her tears and gave him her other hand. The other three judged this a good moment to leave the room. They came out of the cottage and shut the door behind them. Freddy and Gertie looked at Tatty warily. She gave a great sigh.

'Well,' she said. 'It looks as though I'm not getting married after all.' She considered this for a moment, then said, 'Mother and Father won't be too pleased, but I must say it's something of a relief. Now, we'd better get back to the party.'

And with that she walked off, leaving Freddy and Gertie to glance at each other and follow.

Chapter Nineteen

'I SHALL NEVER get engaged again,' said Gertie. 'It only leads to misery. Still, I'm glad all's well that ends well—and glad, too, that Tatty got him before I did. If *I'd* been engaged to him then I'd have had it all to deal with.'

'I suppose so,' said Freddy absently. She looked at him curiously.

'What is it? You're thinking of something else.'

'I'm just hoping for Irene's sake that Tom Chetwynd didn't murder Douglas Westray,' said Freddy.

'You don't really think he did, do you?'

'He had a big enough motive that night. Douglas was wandering around drunk, dropping loud hints about what Tom had been getting up to. And Tom said himself that with Douglas dead his secret was safe—until now, at any rate, although he couldn't have foreseen what was going to happen today. But no, as it happens, I don't really think Tom killed him. He doesn't have the brains, for a start, and something tells me this murder was a cunning affair. Besides, his story bears out what Colonel Lomas told me at Skeffington's, which is that Douglas went to Tom's flat because he'd discovered something and wanted Tom's advice on what he should do about it. Tom was in no condition to listen, but he did remember that Douglas had said something about someone who'd got away with murder.'

'That's just a figure of speech,' said Gertie.

'True enough, but he said a similar thing to Colonel Lomas, only in slightly different words: he told Lomas that he couldn't decide whether or not to speak up, and that if he didn't then he would be a *party* to murder, which puts an altogether different aspect on it, don't you think?'

Gertie looked sceptical.

'But nobody's been murdered,' she pointed out. 'Apart from Doug, I mean.'

'No, that is the difficulty,' Freddy admitted.

They fell silent, considering the matter, then Gertie gave an exclamation.

'Oh, but there *is* someone!' she said excitedly. 'Don't you remember what Lois told you about Captain Dauncey? He was booted out of the Air Force because of some incident in which two people died. It was thought to be an accident, but what if Douglas had found out that it wasn't?'

'Now that *is* a thought! Yes, perhaps you're onto something there. I wonder, now—I might be able to do a little snooping into his war record and find out what exactly happened. We already know he's up to no good, but the question is: has he taken it as far as murder?'

'I'm sure he must have,' said Gertie. 'He killed these two men, whoever they were, then Doug somehow found out about it and threatened to expose him, so he killed him too.'

'If that's true, we shall have to be very careful. I've already put the wind up him once, remember? I don't want him to have a second go at running me down flat.'

'No, but still, we must work quickly before he decides things are getting too hot around here and disappears,' said Gertie.

But as it transpired, they were too late, for Corky Beckwith had been hard at work on his own version of the story following his adventure in East London, and was all set to steal a march on them. On the Tuesday following the garden-party, the *Herald* ran a big story, hinting in the strongest terms that a certain foreign individual, whose name would not be unfamiliar to regular readers of the company news, had been involved in the incitement of underhand practices to the great detriment of the reputation of the British engineering industry. The *Herald's* correspondent had run no little risk of harm to his own person in his zeal to uncover the truth, and had ascertained in the course of his investigations that a certain company, Stamboul Export Co, had been secretly employing people to spy on large engineering companies, and in some instances, perform despicable acts of sabotage on their machines. Further inquiry had revealed that Stamboul Export Co. was an indirect subsidiary of the world-renowned engineering firm Rawson Welbeck, and that its chief executive officer was Mr. Anatoli Salmanov, who, readers would remember, had been named as one of the leading figures in the Celebes copper mining scandal, although no action was ever brought against him.

Further, the paper's correspondent regretted to say that a deeper examination of the matter had revealed that a certain person closely associated with the field of aviation, whose name had for many years been on the lips of everyone in the country thanks to his heroic exploits in the air during the war, was in the pay of Stamboul Export Co, and had been employed by them to engage in acts of industrial espionage and sabotage. The latest example of this had taken place in full view of everyone who had attended the Heston air show less than two weeks ago, when a new fighter aircraft developed by the Nugent Corporation had failed in mid-air, and disaster had, to all appearances, narrowly been avoided. However, the *Herald's* correspondent was in a position to state with authority that the pilot of the plane had, in fact, tampered with its engine himself—a perilous act indeed, for only a pilot of his daring and expertise would have risked flying the machine while it was in such a state. It was not to be supposed that Rawson Welbeck was cognisant of what was going on at its subsidiary, but questions were bound to be asked. The *Herald* did not name the famous pilot, but there was no need to, for it was perfectly obvious whom it was talking about.

Freddy was reading the article eagerly on Tuesday morning when Gertie swept in and up to his desk, brandishing her own copy of the paper.

'Have you seen the news in the *Herald* this morning?' she demanded.

'*I* have, but what are you doing, buying the *Herald*? Don't mention it too loudly or old Bickerstaffe will peg you as an enemy of all right-thinking people and run unflattering stories about you.'

'Silly—the head footman gets it and lets me read it. But have you seen what it says about Dauncey? He sabotaged the plane himself! Can it be true?'

'It had better be, or the *Herald* is going to be in deep trouble. No, even Corky isn't that stupid. I can only suppose he must have found some solid evidence that Dauncey nobbled the plane, or they'd never have let him run the story.'

'True enough. Oh, Freddy, can there be any doubt now that he murdered Doug? Doug must have known that Dauncey was up to no good and told him so, and Dauncey killed him to keep him quiet.' Her face fell. 'Oh, but that means Lois must have been in on it too. If she was with Dauncey on the balcony then she must have been lying about his not going through the window.'

'No, I don't think she was lying.'

'But then how did he get in to kill Doug?'

'As a matter of fact, I've been thinking about that. What do you say to a walk?'

'A walk? Where to.'

'Tatty's house.'

'Can't we just telephone her?'

'I don't want to speak to her. I want to see something.'

Despite her badgering he refused to answer any more of her questions, and persisted in whistling exasperatingly all the way to St. James's Square.

'This had better be good,' said Gertie darkly as they went up the steps and Freddy knocked smartly on the Browncliffes' front door. It was answered at length by Sally, the maid.

'Miss Patricia is out with her ladyship, and Mr. Whitcomb isn't here,' she said doubtfully, upon their request to enter the house.

'He won't mind. And nor will Miss Patricia,' said Freddy. 'I promise I'll take full responsibility for it and won't let Gertie steal the silver, even though she's rather inclined that way.'

'Ass,' said Gertie, and went in without waiting for any further invitation.

'May we go up to her ladyship's dressing-room?' said Freddy.

'It's locked, sir,' said Sally.

'Do you know where the key is kept?'

Sally did know, but had misgivings. On further promises from Freddy that she would not get into trouble for any of this, she was persuaded to fetch it, and they all went upstairs.

'You may stay and watch if you like,' said Freddy.

He glanced around the room. Gertie and Sally were gazing at him expectantly.

'Go on, then,' said Gertie. 'If he didn't use the window, then how did he get in—or out, rather?'

'Through the door, of course,' said Freddy.

'But it was locked on the inside.'

'It was *bolted* on the inside, which is quite a different thing.' He turned to the china plates that were hanging on the wall by the door and indicated the blue and gold one with the flowers. 'When we got in through the window and discovered Douglas's body, this plate was on the floor, standing against the wall.

Whitcomb saw it and hung it back up, thinking it had fallen down because of the shot, but in actual fact it had been taken down deliberately.'

He took down the plate carefully and leaned it against the wall again.

'You see this hook?' he said. 'Notice that it's at the same height as the bolt on the door.'

'What of it?' said Gertie.

Freddy turned and crossed to the little table on which Lady Browncliffe's sewing-box was standing, gathering dust.

'I need a needle and thread,' he said. He peered into the box and took out a bobbin of pink silk embroidery thread, then selected a long needle. 'And a hook of some sort. A bent pin might do it, or some wire—aha! I see we have some ready-made ones.' He brought out a small card of metal hooks. 'One missing, I see. Not that that proves anything—after all, Lady Browncliffe might have used it herself.'

He took some scissors and cut a long length of the pink thread, then fastened the hook to one end of it. The other end he threaded through the needle.

'I remember playing a trick of the sort at school,' he said. 'I've been trying it at home, but it doesn't work very well because the only bolt I have is too stiff. The bolt on this door slides easily, though, so it might work. Now, watch. We hook this end onto the bolt fastener—' he suited the action to the word, '—then pass the thread around the plate hook, keeping it taut. Then the needle goes through the keyhole, like so. You see? The plate hook acts as a kind of pulley. Now, I duck outside the door and close it, still keeping the thread taut.'

He squeezed out through the almost-closed door and shut it behind him.

'Now, look what happens when I pull on the needle,' came his voice from the other side of the door.

Gertie and Sally watched in fascination as the bolt slid across and into its fastening.

'Did it work?' called Freddy.

'I'll say!' said Gertie.

'Now all I have to do is let the thread go slack and the hook should fall off the bolt.'

He demonstrated, and they watched as the thread and the hook disappeared through the keyhole.

'Well I never!' exclaimed Sally. 'It's like magic!'

'Let me in, won't you?' said Freddy.

Gertie unbolted the door, her eyes shining.

'I believe you've got it!' she said. 'So nobody went through the window at all! Here, let me try.'

After one or two fumbling attempts she, too, succeeded in bolting the door from the outside, then Sally was allowed to try it. It seemed clear that this was how the murder had been done, and how the killer had made Douglas's death look like suicide.

'We've been looking at the wrong part of the house all along,' said Gertie. 'We ought to have been asking who went upstairs, rather than who went onto the balcony.'

'Yes, and it might have been anyone,' said Freddy.

'Oh, but it must have been Dauncey.'

'I'm inclined to think it was. But I'd still like to know what happened to Douglas's shoes.'

'Does it matter? It's not important, surely.'

'Perhaps not, but I don't like things to remain unexplained.'

'Well, we can think about it afterwards,' said Gertie. 'Now that we've got a motive, and we know that Dauncey was up to no good, all we have to do is find some proof that he came in here.'

'Easier said than done.'

'We'll think of something, I'm sure,' said Gertie.

They took their leave of Sally and came out, to find Corky Beckwith loitering outside the house.

'Not you again,' said Gertie. 'What is it this time? Have you come to ask where I buy my stockings?'

'Not at all, not at all,' said Corky. 'I'm merely passing the time on this beautiful day. There's nothing like a spot of sunshine to fill the heart with gladness and joy, don't you think?'

'Rot. I suppose you're looking for a story again. Well, you won't find one.'

'Then you have nothing to tell about any impending nuptials? I must say, the two of you seem inseparable lately. I never see one of you without the other. Tell me, when can we expect an announcement? Speaking of which, a little bird tells me that the much-vaunted and wildly fêted betrothal between two people of your close acquaintance is about to come to naught. I don't suppose you'd care to expand upon the subject?'

'No,' said Freddy.

'Pity. News is a little sparse on the social side of things, although Lord knows I've plenty of other news to keep me going. I suppose you saw my piece this morning, Freddy? First off the mark again, you'll note. You really ought to try harder to keep up. But that's what you get for employing Lady Gertrude to do your dirty work for you. Very decorative, the ladies, but lacking in mental acuity as a rule. No,' he went on blithely, before Gertie could formulate a trenchant interjection, 'one doesn't like to boast, but I rather think I've come out well in this story. I have a series of follow-ups planned for the rest of the week. The police have taken an interest, you know. They searched the offices of Stamboul Export Co, and have found a whole set-up, with spies planted in dozens of companies here and abroad. Of course, it will be difficult to prove Rawson Welbeck knew anything about it, although the fact of their having employed Anatoli Salmanov indicates it was deliberate.'

'But what about Captain Dauncey?' said Gertie. 'How can you be sure he won't sue you for libel?'

'He may try if he likes,' said Corky. 'But since you ask, I don't think the *Herald* will be troubled with legal action, since we've had word this morning that Dauncey has "done a bunk," as the vulgar saying goes. I've found a witness who is prepared to sign a statement to the effect that on the day of the air show he was paid to keep a look-out while Dauncey sabotaged the Nugent Nuthatch shortly before take-off, and I dare say that's what has spurred him to this present action.'

'He's disappeared?' said Gertie in dismay. 'You idiot! You've driven him off just when we were about to prove he killed Douglas!'

Freddy nudged her sharply, but it was too late, for Corky had pricked up his ears immediately.

'Douglas?' he said. 'Do you mean Douglas Westray? Surely that was suicide?'

'Of course it was suicide. Gertie didn't mean it literally,' said Freddy quickly. 'She thinks they might have had a row that contributed to Westray's depressed state of mind, that's all.'

'That's right,' said Gertie, recollecting herself. 'I meant what Freddy said.'

'Is that so?' said Corky, regarding them both narrowly. 'Hmm, I shall have to look into that. Perhaps I can lay another charge at his door and stretch the story out for day or two.'

'That's right, kick a man when he's down,' said Freddy. 'It's a pity they stopped hanging people in public, isn't it?'

'Oh, yes,' agreed Corky with perfect sincerity.

Freddy glanced at his watch.

'Well, it's been delightful to pass the time, old chap, but I must get back to the office,' he said.

Gertie was also wanted back at home, and so they parted for the present. Corky dithered over whether to pester Freddy all the way back to Fleet Street or follow Gertie, and eventually decided on the latter. Freddy callously left her to Corky's tender mercies and set off back to the *Clarion's* offices. It was exasperating that Corky had driven Dauncey away just when they had been starting to make material progress in the investigation, but when all was said and done it did look very much as though Dauncey were a guilty man, and in any case there was nothing that could be done for the present until he was found, so Freddy returned to work and tried to forget about the matter, supposing that the case had at least reached some sort of conclusion, even if no-one had been arrested.

Sure enough, the *Herald* ran a series of stories about the sabotage scandal, as it was being called, over the next few days, and each one showed Captain Dauncey in a worse light than before. Soon, the whole country was talking about it, and shaking their heads over the fall from grace of their former hero. There were those who said that Dauncey's brave feats ought not to be forgotten, however far he had sunk since, but most people were quite happy to forget they had ever admired him, and to condemn him as a traitor and the worst of men.

On Thursday, Freddy was sitting in the office, reading over some notes with a dissatisfied air, when Jolliffe came in, looking busy.

'Can't stop,' he said. 'I'm going to be late for the Finkley inquest.'

'Eh? What's that?' said Freddy absently.

'You know, the woman who was flattened by a car at the air show. Hilda Finkley, her name was. Very unfortunate, and all because of the crowds, I understand.'

Freddy looked up and frowned.

'Hilda Finkley—now, where have I heard that name before?' he said.

'Couldn't tell you, old chap. Let me know when you remember, but not now. Must dash!'

With that he rushed off, and Freddy went back to his work. After a minute he sat up straight, for he had just remembered Hilda Finkley. She was the engineer's widow he had spoken to on the day of the air show. She must have died only an hour or two after he had spoken to her. What an odd coincidence. He reflected briefly and poignantly on the vagaries of Fate, then returned again to his notes. But his work was destined to be left unfinished, for once again a memory darted into his brain and he straightened up in his chair.

'Now, what the devil—?' he murmured.

He frowned over the thought for a while. It could not be a coincidence, surely, although he could not see how exactly it fitted into the mystery. Still, there was no concentrating on his work while the thing was on his mind. He reached a decision and made a short telephone-call, then replaced the receiver and stared straight ahead for several minutes.

'How very odd,' he said at last.

Chapter Twenty

FREDDY WAS KEPT busy for most of that afternoon, and so was unable to spare the time to pursue his line of thought, but he watched the door anxiously, waiting for Jolliffe to return to the office, for he wished to consult him. At a quarter past three, Jolliffe returned, and gave Freddy the information he was looking for, not without some curiosity. At five o'clock Freddy left the office to set off for an address on the Caledonian Road—a trim, terraced house with a red front door, at which he knocked, and asked to speak to a Mrs. Wade. The lady in question was in, and after a little hesitation was persuaded to speak to him. Some time later he emerged from the house and headed back into town on foot, for it was a very fine evening. When he reached the bottom of Gray's Inn Road he hesitated, undecided, then bent his footsteps towards Lincoln's Inn Fields, where he sat on a bench, took out his notebook and spent some time writing down what he had learnt. There were still several things which were not wholly clear to him—the shoes in particular—but he was now almost certain that he knew who had murdered Douglas Westray, and why. Knowing was one thing, however, but proving it was quite another, and he had no idea how to do that, for it seemed to him that the only way to find evidence would be to convince the police that Douglas's death had not been suicide after all, and for them to obtain a search-warrant and seek the evidence themselves.

He did not hold out much hope that the police would be prepared to act, but he decided to try anyway. He sought out a telephone box and telephoned Sergeant Bird at Scotland Yard. The sergeant listened to his story with interest, and, far from pooh-poohing it, was inclined to think that Freddy was on to something. But as Freddy had feared, since the inquest had come down so firmly in favour of suicide, there was little he could do, he said, without some strong evidence that foul play had been involved. Since evidence was just what Freddy did not have, there was nothing to do but bid the sergeant good evening and hang up. Then he continued on his way home, still absorbed in his own thoughts. He was so busy cogitating as he went that as he turned a corner he almost cannoned into a cart on which many crates of eggs were balanced precariously. The delivery-man had stopped to remove something from one of his horse's hooves, and, fortunately for all concerned, was able to shout a warning just in time, before disaster occurred. Freddy begged pardon and passed by hurriedly, but was vexed, because he was sure the incident had interrupted an important train of thought, and that he had been on the point of making a very important deduction. He could not for the life of him bring it back to mind, and in the end decided to leave it, for he knew that trying too hard to remember something was the surest way to fail in the attempt. He had not got ten yards farther on, however, before he stopped short and turned to look back. He stared at the horse and cart for several minutes.

'I wonder if that's it,' he said to himself. 'Yes, that would make sense. But what was it?'

He returned to the *Clarion's* offices, where he spent some time reading through the archives and frowning, until one of his colleagues found him and asked if he was feeling quite well, for it was almost unheard of for Freddy to be still in the office at this time. It was getting late, and he had found out what he was looking for, so he went home and was just in time to catch Gertie on the telephone before she went out for the evening.

'What are you doing tomorrow night?' he said.

'I was supposed to be going out with Priss and her latest,' she said. 'Not that I particularly want to play gooseberry, but everybody else is away.'

'Come to dinner with me instead. I've been tremendously clever and I need a woman to clasp her hands together and gaze at me admiringly.'

'I can't promise to do that, but of course I'll come out with you—anything's better than watching Priss and whatever he's called going soppy over each other all night. What is it? Don't tell me you've tracked Captain Dauncey down to his lair?'

'I fear you must restrain your curiosity for now, my child. Wait until tomorrow, and I'll tell you all.'

'Bother, I hate waiting.'

'It'll be worth it, I promise,' he said, and hung up.

The next night Freddy quite infuriatingly refused to say a word until dinner was finished—on the grounds, he said, that if he had to talk his lamb-chops would go cold—so Gertie was once again kept on tenterhooks. But after coffee had been served and he had smoked two cigarettes and was wondering aloud whether to have a *digestif*, Gertie could contain herself no longer.

'Freddy!' she exclaimed. 'If you don't tell me what this mystery is all about this instant I swear I shall throttle you with my own hands here in front of everybody.'

'How impatient are the younger generation,' he said sententiously. She glared at him. 'Oh, very well, then. Listen, and then tell me how marvellous I am. Now, where shall I start? I'll tell you how I reached my conclusions, and, as an extra gesture of generosity I shall also tell you that there was one thing you were right about—incidentally, have I mentioned how fetching you look in that frock? You ought to wear duck-egg blue more often.'

'Get on with it, you ass.'

'Some women *like* a compliment. All right, then: you remember the Heston air show?'

'Yes.'

'Well, on that day I was doing my job as a hard-working press-man and mingling with the crowds, taking photographs and all that. While I was doing that I fell into conversation with a woman called Hilda Finkley, who told me at rather tedious length that she was the widow of an inventor. She was a talkative sort, so I let her rattle on and took a few notes just for the look of the thing, then forgot all about her. I later heard from Jolliffe that on that very day, not long after she'd talked to me, she was run down by a motor-car and killed.'

'Goodness!'

'Quite. Now, you may remember that a very similar thing happened to me on that day. I was coming home late in the evening and a car headed straight for me, and it was only by a stroke of very good luck that I wasn't squashed to a pulp. I didn't think anything of it at the time, and assumed it was a coincidence, but then yesterday when Jolliffe told me he was going to the inquest into Mrs. Finkley's death, I suddenly remembered that I'd heard the name Finkley before, on the night of the dance. I remembered he was something to do with Westray Enterprises, so I called them to find out, and they said that Hector Finkley was an inventor who had worked for Westray for many years until he died. Naturally I wondered whether there was a connection, so I asked Jolliffe when he came back. He told me firstly that Hilda Finkley was Hector Finkley's widow, and secondly that Mrs. Finkley's death had been a hit-and-run accident, and that the driver had never been traced.

'At that point all sorts of questions began springing up in my head. It couldn't really be a coincidence that both of us had been involved in car accidents on the same day, could it? I knew that in my case it had been deliberate, so I wondered whether it was the same driver who'd run over Hilda Finkley. But why? The only thing I could think of was that Hilda Finkley knew something, that we'd been seen together, and that someone must have been afraid that she'd told me—whatever it was. The thing is, she hadn't said anything of interest to me that I could recall. I looked at my notes and found I'd scrawled a few words that didn't seem to mean much, except for one suggestive phrase to the effect that Mrs. Finkley's late husband had left behind him a notebook of inventions. It probably wasn't important, but I thought there couldn't be any harm in looking into it. I found out from Jolliffe that the Finkleys had a married daughter, so I waited until I thought she'd had time to get home from the inquest and then paid her a visit. She told me one or two curious things, the first being that her father died last year after falling from a balcony in one of the workshops at the Westray factory, and the second being that her mother had found Finkley's notebook among his things quite recently, and had taken it to Douglas Westray the week before he died, thinking the company might find it useful. Of course, there was no reason to suppose anything untoward had happened—except that I telephoned the Westray factory and the Westrays' house, and found that not only did nobody know where this notebook was, nobody had even heard of its existence. It was certainly not among Douglas's possessions.'

'So where is it?'

'A very good question. And there are plenty of other questions, too: what was in the notebook, for example? Also, was Finkley's death really an accident, or was he murdered?'

'Murdered! But who would want to murder him?'

'Someone who wanted his ideas, presumably.'

Gertie stared.

'Do you mean—?' she said, then stopped.

'Leslie Penbrigg, yes,' said Freddy.

'That harmless idiot?' said Gertie. 'I know I suspected him for half a minute, but have you seen him dripping around Alida?'

'Yes,' said Freddy, 'but I also knew him at school. He may be useless around women, but he was absolutely ruthless when it came to his contraptions—quite happy to destroy other people's things in order to get what he wanted. I never knew such a single-minded fellow. I don't know for certain, but I can make a guess at what happened. Finkley died last year, a few months before the Woodville Prize. What if it was he rather than Penbrigg who came up with the wing slot idea? After all, he was a good deal older and had much more experience than Penbrigg did in aeroplane design. Penbrigg saw the idea was going to be very important and lucrative, and would get him lots of credit, so he saw his chance. I read about the inquest into Finkley's death—there were no witnesses, so who's to say he wasn't pushed from that balcony? By all accounts he was an absent-minded, trusting old buffer, and wouldn't have suspected a thing. A quick shove from behind and Penbrigg could steal all the glory from his former mentor.'

'Isn't that rather far-fetched?'

'Perhaps, when taken by itself. But not quite so far-fetched when taken together with all the other circumstances of the case. We know Mrs. Finkley brought a notebook to Douglas, and Douglas was murdered shortly afterwards. I suspect the notebook contained Finkley's early designs for the wing slot, and was proof that Penbrigg hadn't invented it himself. Presumably Penbrigg hadn't known about Finkley's notebook before, or he would have tried to get hold of it when he killed Finkley. I think what happened was this: Hilda Finkley found the notebook more than a year after her husband's death and brought it quite innocently to Douglas, who forgot about it for a few days—he was away from the office that week, you remember. Then at some point he remembered it and looked through it, and discovered that it was Hector Finkley who had come up with the new wing slot design, and not Leslie Penbrigg at all. He thought about it, and came to the same conclusion I did: namely, that Penbrigg had stolen the design deliberately. He also began to wonder whether Finkley's death had been an accident. On the night of the dance, therefore, he left the house at five o'clock and went to see Penbrigg at the Westray factory, where he let him know of his suspicions. I don't know what Penbrigg said in reply—I expect he denied everything and tried to put Douglas off, but he must have got an awful shock to discover that there was written evidence of his theft.

'After their talk, Douglas locked the notebook in his drawer, came away then went to Tom Chetwynd's flat, because he wanted to ask his friend's advice about what he ought to do. Westray Enterprises had already lost the credit for the wing slot invention after Dauncey stole the design, so there seemed little sense in making a big commotion about it, and attaching scandal to the Westray name. But there was still the question of Finkley. Tom was in no condition to give any advice that evening, as he'd just heard from Irene, so then Douglas went to Skeffington's, where he got roaring drunk and confided rather incoherently in Colonel Lomas. There was no proof of murder, of course—and little chance that any proof would ever be found, since there were no witnesses to Finkley's death—but Douglas knew Penbrigg was in love with Alida, and couldn't let his sister marry a man who was quite possibly a killer. Colonel Lomas told me his exact words. He said: "If I speak up then it'll cause the most terrible stink—and what if I'm wrong? But if I don't then I'm party to murder, and I couldn't do that to the old girl." By old girl he meant Alida. Then after his conversation with Lomas he went to the dance, and behaved just as one would expect in the circumstances.

'Meanwhile, Penbrigg had realized the danger he was in even before he left the factory, and decided he had better be prepared. When he got to the dance and saw Douglas's condition he knew the danger was even more acute, and so he got ready to put his plan into action. I think it was he who listened to the conversation between Douglas and Tatty in the smoking-room, because he wanted to be sure that Douglas hadn't given the game away. When Douglas came out Penbrigg went into the library, took the revolver from the case and loaded it, then sought Douglas out and said he wanted to speak to him about Finkley in private. Douglas quite unsuspectingly took him upstairs to Lady Browncliffe's dressing-room, which he knew had a bolt on it, and locked the door behind them. I expect he thought Penbrigg was going to give him some explanation or other, but instead Penbrigg shot him and escaped back through the door, using the needle and thread trick I showed you before.'

Gertie, who had been listening open-mouthed, now shook her head, unconvinced.

'But how did he plan so quickly to make it look like suicide? How could he have known there was a bolt on the door, for example, or that Lady Browncliffe had a sewing-box in the room?'

'Oh, he didn't. His first thought was to put Douglas out of the way as quickly as possible, then slip out of the room. As long as nobody heard the shot, then there was a good chance he could be at the other end of the house by the time the body was found—or even at home, if it wasn't found until after the dance—and with any luck everybody would think Douglas had died by his own hand.'

'That's another thing: why *did* nobody hear the shot? I've been wondering about that.'

'He used a home-made silencer on the gun,' said Freddy. 'I saw it in his pocket, but I wasn't paying much attention and thought it was a toy whistle, so I didn't think anything of it. When he showed me around his workshop I saw more of them. He's been working on a new type of engine muffler, so knows all about how to make them. I think that when Douglas confronted him at the factory a desperate plan was already beginning to form in his mind. He, like everybody, knew about Lord Browncliffe's gun collection, so he brought a silencer with him to the dance, thinking it might come in useful. The police doctor told me he thought the gun had been fired from a few inches away, and the silencer explains why. At any rate, Penbrigg shot Douglas, removed the silencer and staged the scene, and was just about to slip out of the room when he saw the sewing-box and the plate near the door, and the idea came to him to bolt the door from the inside and make it seem absolutely clear that it was suicide. This he did, and very successfully, as we know.

'As soon as he could after the dance, he went to the Westray factory, broke into Douglas's drawer and stole the notebook, and congratulated himself on a job well done. But then on the day of the air show he saw me talking to Mrs. Finkley, and shortly afterwards I asked him some asinine question about whether all the inventions on display were his own work. Later on I ran around asking everybody about Douglas's shoes. No wonder he got the wind up—he must have thought Mrs. F. had come to me with compromising information, and decided to put us both out of the way. You said he was looking shifty when he saw us, and I dare say he was.'

'Where *do* the shoes come in, by the way?' said Gertie. 'You've been harping on about them for weeks. Are they important?'

'Yes, I believe they are. I think Penbrigg swapped them for his own after the murder. This is guess-work, mind, but I have an idea about them. I got it from a horse.'

'What?'

'The floor of Penbrigg's workshop is covered with metal shavings and suchlike. I think that when Douglas went there he got something stuck in his shoe—something that would have given away the fact that he'd been to the Westray factory shortly before he died. When we found his body he was sprawled in a chair, and I think Penbrigg noticed it as he was about to leave the room and realized it could give him away. If there was an investigation, and the police spotted whatever it was, then there was a chance they would realize Douglas must have picked it up that night, since the shoes were new, and that they'd then go straight to the factory and find the notebook in Douglas's drawer before Penbrigg could get it. It wasn't *very* likely, but there was no sense in running the risk. First he tried to get the thing out of the shoe using the pen nib and Lady Browncliffe's comb, but whatever it was must have been stuck fast, so in the end he swapped his own shoes for Douglas's before leaving the room. Then he spent the rest of the evening hobbling around in a pair of shoes that were two sizes two small for him.'

'Goodness me!' said Gertie, astonished. She pondered for some moments. 'He's ruthless, all right. I wonder why he didn't try and kill you again after the first attempt failed.'

'I imagine he would have tried it if he'd had the chance, although he couldn't be absolutely sure I knew anything.'

Gertie laughed.

'He must have been sick when Westray lost the Woodville Prize after he'd gone to all the trouble of killing Finkley!'

'Yes—and it's ironic, too, that he stole a design and in turn had it stolen from him. But that also gave him an additional reason for killing Douglas, because he'd have taken all the credit for the wing slot design had Douglas not forgotten to register the patent. Now, this is the part where you flutter your eyelashes at me and tell me how clever I've been.'

'Yes, you have been clever,' Gertie said. 'But you look just like Corky when you're pleased with yourself.'

'Heaven forbid!' said Freddy in disgust. 'Still, though, it's all very well knowing what happened, but I don't know what to do next. I've already spoken to the police about it, and they said there's nothing they can do without evidence. The inquest is over and done with, and as far as they're concerned it was suicide, so they're not going to hare off on a wild-goose chase. Can one goose off on a wild-hare chase, I wonder?'

'Idiot. But we must do something. We can't just let him get away with it. Where do you think he keeps the notebook?'

'I expect he's destroyed it,' said Freddy gloomily.

'No, he won't have destroyed it—it's full of Finkley's ideas, remember? He won't be able to resist keeping it and seeing if there's anything else he can steal for himself. I'll bet it's locked up somewhere in his workshop.'

'By Jove, I shouldn't wonder if you're right! Yes, that would make much more sense. But we'll never find out unless we can persuade the police to search the place, and how can we do that?'

'We'll just have to think of a way,' said Gertie.

Chapter Twenty-One

THEY LEFT THE restaurant and then went on to a night-club, where they passed a pleasant hour or two. The music was lively, the place was crowded with fashionable people, and there was plenty to observe and comment upon without any thoughts of murder intruding to spoil their enjoyment. Their revelry was not destined to continue, however, for they were sitting at their table and considering a dance when Gertie's eyes widened suddenly.

'Look!' she said.

She nodded at something over Freddy's shoulder. Freddy turned and saw that Alida Westray was just entering the night-club, followed, to his astonishment, by Leslie Penbrigg himself.

'Well, I'll be damned! So the old chap has finally plucked up the courage to speak,' murmured Freddy, momentarily forgetting that the 'old chap' in question was quite possibly a murderer.

Alida had spotted them, and was seen in consultation with Penbrigg, and at length they were seated at the table next to Freddy and Gertie's.

'We went to the theatre to see that new play, and then had a very late dinner,' said Alida. 'The play was rather good, wasn't it, Leslie?'

'Oh—er—rather,' said Leslie Penbrigg, who did not appear to have become any less tongue-tied.

Alida seemed in a chatty mood. She spent some time telling them about the play, then said, as though she had just remembered:

'By the way, Freddy, I thought Father might know something about that notebook you mentioned, so I asked him this morning, but he said he knew nothing about it.'

At her words Freddy and Gertie froze momentarily, then Gertie kicked Freddy under the table as Leslie Penbrigg looked up.

'Which notebook?' he said. He spoke in his usual pleasant manner, and his face wore an expression of mild curiosity.

'You remember Mr. Finkley, don't you?' said Alida, with blithe unawareness that she was saying anything of importance. 'Apparently he left a notebook full of drawings behind him, and Mrs. Finkley gave it to Douglas just before he died. Freddy was wondering what had happened to it.'

Leslie Penbrigg regarded Freddy blandly.

'A notebook of drawings, eh? I expect it's lying around somewhere,' he said.

'Yes, I expect it is,' said Freddy.

There was a short silence, then Gertie said:

'What time is it, Freddy?'

'One o'clock,' he replied.

She gasped.

'Oh, goodness! I promised faithfully I'd be back before midnight. You'd better take me home.'

'What?' said Freddy, surprised, but she was glaring at him meaningfully. 'Oh—er—very well.'

The bill was settled, then they said their goodbyes to Penbrigg and Alida and rose to leave. Gertie stumbled heavily against Penbrigg's chair as they passed.

'Careful, old girl. I told you not to have that third glass of champagne,' said Freddy. They went outside, and he gave a grimace. 'Damn! Of all the rotten luck. Why didn't I think to tell her to keep it quiet? Now he'll know we're after him and he'll hide the thing as soon as he can.'

'Yes, that's what I thought,' said Gertie. 'That's why I stole his keys. Now we can go and search his workshop.'

Freddy regarded her in astonishment. Sure enough, she was holding up a bunch of keys and looking very pleased with herself.

'Good Lord! Is that what you were doing when you were lumbering about in there? Picking his pocket?'

'Rather a good job on my part, don't you think?' said Gertie.

'Remind me to introduce you to a friend of mine,' said Freddy.

'Who's that? Never mind, there's no time. Let's go!'

'What, now? You're not exactly suitably dressed for breaking and entering.'

'Nor are you, for that matter, but we haven't a minute to lose! We have to get the notebook before Penbrigg does.'

Before he could object she had flagged down a taxi and jumped in.

'Take me to the aeroplane factory,' she said grandly. 'I don't know where it is.'

The taxi driver turned an appealing gaze on Freddy.

'Hammersmith,' said Freddy.

'And make it quick,' said Gertie.

The taxi pulled away, and in a very short time they had reached their destination. The driver set them down on King Street, since they did not wish to draw attention to themselves, and they alighted and set off on the short walk to the factory.

'How are we going to get in through the gate?' said Gertie as they walked. 'I expect there'll be a night-watchman.'

'Yes, and I don't suppose he'll just let us in through the front door.' Freddy was trying to remember what he had seen on his last visit. Penbrigg's workshop had been in a back yard surrounded by high walls. 'I think there might be a back gate,' he said. 'We'll just have to hope one of these keys fits.'

They had now passed into a quiet area which was unlit by street-lamps. It was dark, but the moon was not long past full, which allowed them to see where they were going. They arrived at the front gates of the factory and peeped through. The windows were in darkness, but one light had been left on over the entrance.

'Can't see anyone,' said Freddy at last. 'Let's go and find a back gate. This way.'

They turned right and entered a tiny alley which skirted the boundary of the factory. Here the moonlight could not penetrate and it was much darker. After a few yards Freddy stopped.

'I think the workshop is about here,' he said. He looked up. 'Hmm. An eight-foot wall with broken glass along it. Nothing doing there. Now, is there a gate or not?'

'Of course there's a gate,' said Gertie. 'There must be.'

They carried on along the alley and then turned left, still following the factory wall. Here the alley became a narrow path, bounded on one side by thick bushes.

'There it is!' she hissed.

Sure enough, a little farther ahead, the wall was broken by a solid wooden gate, which was firmly shut. A man in a uniform and peaked cap was leaning against the gate, idly playing a torch over the bushes and smoking a cigarette. As they watched, the torch beam headed towards them, and they ducked hurriedly back into the alley.

'Bother!' whispered Gertie. 'Now what do we do?'

'Wait for him to finish his cigarette, I suppose.'

They waited. After a minute or two, Freddy peeped around the corner, and to his shock and dismay saw that the night-watchman was only a few yards away, heading towards them. He had approached so quietly that they had not heard him. He withdrew his head immediately and grabbed Gertie's arm, then indicated with frantic gestures that it was time to retreat. Gertie gave a silent gasp and glanced towards the entrance of the alley, preparing to make a run for it. But there was no time: the darkness was already becoming thinner as the torch beam approached, and they could hear the man clearing his throat. He could not be more than a few yards away. It was too late to escape now. There was no alternative; desperate measures were required. Without ceremony Freddy pulled Gertie towards him.

'Sorry,' he said hastily, and kissed her.

The night-watchman rounded the corner, gave an appreciative snigger as he passed, and walked off, breaking into a cheery whistle as he did so. Freddy let Gertie go. There was a short, breathless silence.

'Are you *quite* sure it wasn't Mungo?' she said at last.

'I suppose it might have been,' said Freddy.

'Do it again, just to make sure.'

Freddy obliged.

'Well, this is all splendid fun, but we are here for a reason,' she said after a little while. 'Hadn't we better go and try the gate before he comes back?'

'Ah, yes,' said Freddy, recollecting himself.

The night-watchman was nowhere to be seen, so he let her go and they returned to the gate, Gertie smoothing down her frock and fighting an inclination to giggle. She brought out the keys from her handbag and they picked the one that looked most likely. Freddy tried it, and after a little struggle it turned in the lock. Gertie beamed at him in excitement and pushed at the gate, which creaked slightly. On the other side was the overgrown yard which Freddy had already seen on the day he visited Penbrigg.

'It's over here,' he whispered. He took her hand and they crept across to the low building inside which was Penbrigg's workshop. The keys were produced again and an entry effected.

The waning moon cast a thin light through the small windows, and as far as Freddy could see in the dim light, the place was as untidy as ever.

'A torch would be preferable, but I'm afraid we'll have to make do with the moonlight,' he said. 'Be careful where you put your feet.'

'I see what you mean about all the scraps of metal on the floor,' said Gertie, picking her way gingerly across the room. 'Now, where shall we look first?'

'I suggest the drawers.'

It was not easy to search in the near-darkness, but they did their best. Most of the drawers were not locked, but there was such a jumble of things inside them that it quickly became clear it would be almost impossible to find anything in the time available to them, unless they had a stroke of good luck. After a fruitless search lasting several minutes, Gertie began trying the doors of the cupboards. She opened one and found it was full of piles of loose paper, jars of screws, twisted bits of metal and machine parts, but nothing that looked like a notebook. She tried the next one.

'Oh, this one is locked,' she said. 'Do we have the key to this cupboard?'

Freddy looked up from the drawer he was searching and came over to see. There was a small key which looked as though it might fit. He tried it, and it turned easily in the lock. He opened the door, and gave an exclamation.

'Well, well, what do we have here?' he said, bringing something out. It was a pair of men's shoes.

'Doug's shoes!' said Gertie.

Freddy turned them over and took them across to the window to examine the soles.

'I rather wonder sometimes whether I'm not a genius,' he said.

Gertie looked. Wedged tightly into the heel was a small piece of metal, with the word 'Westray' clearly stamped on it.

'Sparking plug electrode,' said Freddy. 'He said they kept snapping off. I don't suppose the police would have had the sense to realize that Douglas must have picked it up that evening since the shoes were new, but he couldn't take any chances.'

'Now for the notebook.' Gertie went back to the cupboard and rummaged around. 'Nothing,' she said, disappointed. 'Is there anything on the top shelf? I can't reach.'

Freddy put his hand up and felt about, then brought down a sheaf of papers. In among them was a battered old notebook without a cover. He took it across to the window and squinted at it closely. The paper was squared, and was covered with drawings and diagrams and notes. He flicked through the pages.

'Good old Finkley,' he said at last. 'He's even dated his ideas. Aha! Look at this.'

Gertie peered at the page he was indicating.

'What is it? An aeroplane wing?'

'With a slot,' said Freddy. 'And some equations that I shall pretend to understand. And—most importantly of all—a date of August two years ago, some time before the Woodville Prize.'

Gertie took the notebook and began to look through it, then started violently and looked around.

'What is it?' said Freddy.

'Did you hear that noise?' she whispered.

'Which noise?' he said, lowering his voice.

'I don't know. A sort of scraping sound. It came from quite nearby.'

They listened, but heard nothing. Gertie glanced towards the door to Penbrigg's office and pointed. It was slightly ajar. They looked at one another.

'Is it Penbrigg?' whispered Gertie.

Freddy shook his head. There was not time for Penbrigg to have got there before them.

'Just a mouse, I expect,' he said. 'I forgot about that office. I wonder if there's anything else in there we ought to see.'

He went across and pushed the door open, then started back as a shadow loomed up in the darkness.

'You'd have done much better to keep your nose out of things,' said a voice. There was a click and a lamp was switched on, and they gasped as a familiar figure came towards them.

'Captain Dauncey!' exclaimed Gertie.

Chapter Twenty-two

DAUNCEY WAS NOT looking his usual smart, polished self. He had been in hiding for several days now, and appeared tired and slightly unkempt. They were not paying attention to his appearance, however, but to the revolver that was in his hand. He looked astonished when he saw who his intruders were.

'You! What are you two doing here?' he said, but did not lower the gun.

'Well, we weren't looking for you!' said Gertie. 'So this is where you've been hiding. Does Penbrigg know you're here?'

'Of course he does,' said Freddy. 'Well, this is a surprise. I had no idea the two of you were in league. I suppose you've been covering up for him, have you? Or perhaps you even carried out the murder yourself. I assumed it was Penbrigg, but if you're working together then either one of you might have done it.'

Dauncey frowned.

'What are you talking about?' he said. 'I haven't murdered anyone. Who's been murdered?'

'Doug,' said Gertie. 'It wasn't suicide—he was killed deliberately, and if it wasn't you then it was certainly Leslie Penbrigg.'

'Rot,' said Dauncey. 'Douglas killed himself all right.'

'No he didn't, and we have proof!' said Gertie. 'When you next see Penbrigg, ask him why he's hiding Doug's shoes in his cupboard, and how exactly he got hold of them. And while you're at it, ask him how Hector Finkley died. He'll probably tell you it was an accident, but we know better.'

Dauncey was looking at something over her shoulder.

'Is this true?' he said, and they whirled around to see Leslie Penbrigg at the door, still in his evening things. He came into the workshop, and his face was as bland and pleasant as ever.

'I've come to get my keys back,' he said. 'Rather rude of you to steal them and ruin my evening out. I'll take that, if you don't mind.' He went across to Dauncey and took the gun from him. 'Kind of Alida to give the game away. Women can be useful occasionally. Now, my keys, please. And I see you've found the notebook, too. Give it to me.'

Gertie was still holding it. She looked at Freddy.

'You'd better give it to him,' said Freddy.

She grimaced, but stepped forward and handed it to Penbrigg, who glanced at it and tucked it into his side pocket.

'You know, you'd have been much better off keeping out of it, for all our sakes,' said Penbrigg. 'I have a lot to do, and I don't have time for this sort of thing.'

'Just as you didn't have time for Doug,' burst out Gertie. Her voice was a little wobbly, and Freddy was astonished to see tears in her eyes. She set her jaw and went on, 'He was nothing but an inconvenience to you, so you swept him out of the way.'

'He was a nuisance and a bore, yes,' agreed Penbrigg. 'I had plans, you see, and he wanted to stop me, but I couldn't let him do that. If he'd only kept out of it then he'd still be alive. Goodness knows I don't *like* killing people, but sometimes it simply has to be done.'

'He was a dear, and he didn't deserve what you did to him—he certainly didn't deserve to have everyone thinking he'd killed himself when he did nothing of the sort. And poor old Finkley—you pushed him off that balcony, didn't you? Just so you could take the credit for the wing slot idea. And you killed his wife, too, who probably knew nothing about it.'

Penbrigg shrugged carelessly and did not even bother to reply.

Dauncey had been listening closely.

'Is this true?' he said to Penbrigg. 'Did you kill Douglas?'

'What does it matter?' said Penbrigg dismissively. 'He was a fool!'

This seemed to be a revelation to Dauncey.

'So this is the sort of person I'm allying myself with, is it? And just when I thought I couldn't sink any lower. As a matter of fact, I rather liked Douglas. We were friends at one time, but that all stopped when I did something that offended him. He was very protective of Lois, and quite the gentleman—unlike me, you'll say, and rightly so. I'm not exactly proud of it, but

I was in desperate need of money. I'm afraid it lost you the Woodville Prize, old chap,' he went on, addressing Penbrigg. 'But from what I hear now it was never yours to lose anyway. What a fine pair we are!' He gave a short, sardonic laugh. 'A second-rate inventor who murders his rivals, and a second-rate pilot who takes advantage of women for money.'

'Don't call me second-rate!' snapped Penbrigg. It was the most animation he had shown so far. 'Who got you out of trouble when you needed somewhere to hide?'

'Oh, you did,' Dauncey said. He still had that sardonic look on his face. 'And I assure you I'm more than grateful. I'll get you out of the country, just as I promised, and you can sell your inventions—if they *are* your inventions—to Salmanov for as much as he's prepared to pay you. He's generous enough with his funds.'

'Good. Then we leave tonight, as agreed.'

'But what about Alida?' said Gertie.

Penbrigg's brows drew together in a discontented frown.

'She never took me seriously. Nobody ever took me seriously. Not at school, not at Westray, not anywhere. I was always that silly ass Penbrigg who blew things up for fun. People laughed at me, but I knew I should do great things one day. And I did, too.'

'No you didn't,' Freddy said. 'The wing slot was Finkley's idea.'

'But I improved on it,' said Penbrigg heatedly. 'Finkley's plan was all very well, but I made some adjustments he'd never thought of, and made it altogether better. And besides, what does it matter if one takes a few short-cuts? I've plenty of ideas of my own, too. But nobody appreciates clever chaps here in Britain. I shall go abroad where they give more credit, and pay much better too.'

'And what about you?' said Gertie to Dauncey. 'Are you really going to go with him? He's a murderer, but you're not. Why associate with him?'

'What else can I do?' he replied. 'My reputation's in tatters now, and I've nothing to stay for. I've sold my honour to the highest bidder, and I can't buy it back.'

'But you can put things right. You can face up to what you've done. Most people still think you're a hero after what you did in the war. Go and take your medicine, and they'll forgive you.'

He laughed bitterly.

'I'm afraid it's too late, Gertie. I'm a spy and a traitor. They wouldn't forgive that.'

'I hope you're not thinking of changing your mind,' said Penbrigg sharply. 'We've promised them the Nuthatch and we can't let them down.'

'No, I'll do the job all right,' said Dauncey.

'Good, then let's go. We're just wasting time here.' Penbrigg turned to Freddy. 'Well, it's been simply marvellous to see you again, but now it's time to say goodbye.' He raised the gun. 'Sorry and all that, but we need a head start, and you two are getting in the way.'

'Do you mean you're going to kill us?' said Gertie, taken aback. 'That's not very polite. Can't you just tie us up instead?'

'Look here, old man,' said Freddy. 'Shoot me if you like—I dare say I irritated you enough at school, because Lord knows

I irritated everyone else—but leave Gertie alone. She's done nothing.'

'Very chivalrous of you, but impossible, I'm afraid,' said Penbrigg. 'She'd talk.'

'What does it matter? You'll be long gone by the time they find us.'

Penbrigg merely smiled blandly and raised the gun again.

Dauncey said suddenly:

'What's that?'

'What?' said Penbrigg.

'There's someone outside.'

Dauncey strode over to the door and out into the yard. There came the sounds of a scuffle, and Dauncey returned, hauling with him a protesting Corky Beckwith, who, unknown to himself, was a welcome arrival for perhaps the first time in his life.

'Freddy, old chap! Fancy seeing you here,' he began, but Freddy was not listening, for he had seen his opportunity. At the commotion Penbrigg had lowered the gun and was off his guard momentarily. Without a second's hesitation Freddy launched himself at his old school-friend and grabbed his wrist in an attempt to get the gun off him. Penbrigg was caught by surprise, but was stronger than he looked. He kept a firm grip on the revolver, but the impact of Freddy's attack had knocked him off balance, and they both fell heavily against the wall. There was a sharp report as the gun went off, and Corky bleated in terror. Dauncey cast him aside and went to assist Penbrigg, who had dropped the gun, just as Penbrigg lifted his elbow and jabbed it with some force into Freddy's stomach. Freddy fell to his knees, winded. Meanwhile, Corky had seen the gun and was reaching towards it, but Dauncey got to it first and clapped Corky on the side of the head with it. Corky collapsed sideways and began whimpering.

'Let's go!' said Dauncey sharply.

'Give me the gun!' said Penbrigg.

'Never mind that—we'd better go or we'll be late.'

Penbrigg seemed reluctant, but Dauncey evidently had no intention of handing over the gun, so with one contemptuous glance back he left the workshop, followed by Dauncey. Freddy and Corky were both sitting dazed on the floor. Gertie ran across to Freddy, threw her arms around his neck and began to stroke his hair and plant kisses all over his face.

'You're not hurt? Oh, goodness me, I thought he'd shot you!' she exclaimed.

'Just winded, I think. The bullet went into the wall.'

'Oh, good heavens! My poor, darling boy, you were so brave!'

'It was nothing,' said Freddy modestly, as he accepted the attention that was his due.

Corky sat rubbing his head and watching the affecting scene with a scowl.

'Well, I'm glad you two are happy,' he said. 'Never mind that the blackguard almost knocked my brains out through my ear.'

'Would anybody have noticed the difference if he had?' said Freddy. 'Do that again, Gertie, it was rather nice.'

'Hmph,' said Gertie, suddenly remembering where she was and sitting back. 'That's quite enough of *that!* What are we going to do now?'

'We'd better call the police. It's just a pity they took the notebook.'

'Oh, but they didn't,' said Gertie triumphantly. 'It fell out of his pocket while you were fighting, and I kicked it out of the way over there.'

She pointed to a corner of the room, where the notebook, looking even more battered now, was lying under a chair.

'I must say, you've done some jolly quick thinking this evening,' said Freddy, regarding Gertie with approval. He looked about him. 'There's no telephone here, is there? We'd better go and find one and call from there.'

'This is going to be the most tremendous scoop for me,' said Corky, who was recovering and beginning to sound much more like himself.

'Not if I get there first,' said Freddy.

The old smug look stole across Corky's face.

'You won't. *You* came here in a taxi but *I* had the foresight to bring my own car. It's been an expensive evening, all told—I had to sit for hours in that restaurant while you two gazed lovingly into one another's eyes—'

'We did no such thing!' said Gertie indignantly. 'We were having a perfectly sensible conversation.'

'That's not how it looked from where I was sitting. And then there was the night-club. The doorman didn't want to let me in, so I was forced to offer him a supplementary emolument in addition to the entrance fee, which, I regret to say, he was only too pleased to accept. Where is the incorruptible man in these modern times? I fear he is a thing of the past. Still, I'm glad I had the idea of keeping you in sight, especially after what you said about young Douglas Westray's death. I heard everything that was said, and it seems you were right after all.' He glanced at his watch. 'Now, I'd better get back home. If I hurry, I can put something together in time for tomorrow's early evening edition. Don't stay out all night, Lady Gertrude, and especially not with Freddy. I could tell you some tales about him that would make your hair stand on end—or at least they would if they were suitable for a young lady's ears.'

He smiled genially and went out. Freddy and Gertie followed, bringing the notebook with them.

'Drat it,' said Freddy, as they returned along the little alley and saw street-lights ahead of them. 'I do wish they hadn't got away.'

'I wonder where they're going,' said Gertie.

'Well, it's obvious they're leaving the country, and presumably in a plane, but I don't know where they're planning to fly from.'

'If they're going abroad then they could be flying from almost anywhere.'

'No they couldn't!' said Freddy suddenly. 'Don't you remember what Penbrigg said? "We've promised them the Nuthatch." That's it! They're going to steal the Nuthatch and take it abroad with them.'

'Of course! But where is it?'

'I don't know, that's the problem. Yes I do—it's the South of England air show tomorrow, isn't it? Lord Browncliffe was talking about it. That's at Shoreham. The plane must be there!'

They stared at one another eagerly.

'We must stop them before they fly off with it!' said Gertie. 'How can we do that?'

'We could get the police onto it if only we could get to a telephone,' said Freddy, looking around. 'But it appears civilization hasn't reached Hammersmith yet.'

Indeed, there was no sign of a telephone box nearby. Ahead of them on the road they saw Corky getting into his little car.

'Damn Corky,' said Freddy grumpily. 'And he's going to scoop me too, after all that trouble we went to!'

Corky seemed to be having a little difficulty starting the engine, but at last it stuttered into life.

'No he isn't,' said Gertie suddenly. 'I'm going to get his car.'

'What?' said Freddy, but she was not paying attention. She hurried up to Corky and knocked on the window. He opened it and looked at her inquiringly. She gave him her sincerest smile.

'Listen, shouldn't you like the full story?' she said. 'I can give you all the low-down about what happened, and—' she glanced back, as though to make sure Freddy could not hear, then lowered her voice conspiratorially, '—I'll tell you all about me and Freddy too.'

Corky hesitated, then a satisfied smile spread over his face. He opened the door and unfolded himself from the car.

'Very well,' he said, feeling in his pocket for his notebook. 'What is it you have to tell me?'

Gertie drew him away as though to speak to him confidentially.

'Well, there are one or two things I don't think the papers have got *quite* clear,' she said demurely. 'But I'd much rather tell them to the *Herald* than the *Clarion*.'

'You are quite right to do so,' said Corky. 'I'm glad you've seen sense at last, Lady Gertrude.'

'Sense? Don't be ridiculous,' she said, as she nipped past him quick as lightning and jumped into the car. 'Quick, Freddy!'

Freddy had seen what she was about just in time. He jumped in after her, and she pulled away with a screech of tyres, but she had reckoned without the eccentricity of Corky's car, for after fifty yards or so it stalled and juddered to a halt.

'Drat!' she said. 'I can't get it to start again.'

'Here, let me try,' said Freddy. 'On second thoughts, I'll drive. I've just remembered I swore never to let you drive me again after that day we went to Tunbridge Wells and you nearly hit a cow.'

'That wasn't my fault. I had to swerve or I'd have gone into that tree.'

'Remind me to teach you the difference between a road and a field one day. Now, budge over, and quick, before Corky catches up.'

They exchanged places hurriedly, and he managed to get the engine started, and they roared off again, leaving an outraged Corky shaking his fist at them from the pavement and mouthing words they could not hear.

'Gertie,' said Freddy, as they turned out onto King Street, 'you do know that stealing cars is wrong, don't you?'

'*I'm* not the one driving,' said Gertie pointedly. She giggled mischievously. 'Now we're in for it.'

'I wonder how much he'll sue us for.'

'Oh, I'll square it with him. I'll give him a marvellous story when we get back. Exclusive, too!'

'Oughtn't you to be giving me the exclusive?'

'I didn't say it was going to be *true*. I'll make something up. That's what he usually does, isn't it? Well, I shall save him the trouble.'

'You're quite irrepressible,' said Freddy.

'Of course I am,' she said complacently. 'Now, how far is Shoreham?'

CHAPTER TWENTY-THREE

THE MOON WAS sinking as they crossed the river and drove through the dark streets of the Surrey side. There were few cars about and they made good progress, and it seemed no time at all until they were passing through Croydon, and then Crawley. Corky's car was somewhat temperamental, and Freddy had to pay close attention to prevent it from drifting by inclination over to the wrong side of the road. He glanced across at Gertie, who was quiet and appeared to have dozed off. Suddenly she opened her eyes.

'How are we meant to stop them if we do find them?' she said. 'They're the ones with the gun.'

'I've no idea,' admitted Freddy.

The rest of the journey passed in silence. After some time they began to see road signs indicating that they were close to Brighton, and Freddy looked for the road to Shoreham-by-Sea then turned off. They came into the outskirts of the little town, and Freddy drew up by a telephone box.

'We still haven't called the police,' he said. He got out and made a call lasting some few minutes, then came back to the car. 'I'm not sure they understood what I was talking about, but at least I've tried.'

'I expect it's too late,' said Gertie. 'I shouldn't be surprised if they've already gone.'

The darkness was turning to the beginnings of a chilly grey dawn when they arrived at the aerodrome, to find the place already busy with preparations for the air show. They drove up to the large, square building with its tall central tower and alighted from the car. They were immediately stopped by a man in uniform.

'Press,' said Freddy, showing his pass.

'What? At this time?' said the man, gazing at their evening clothes with the greatest suspicion.

'We want to get the best seats,' explained Freddy. Gertie nodded brightly in agreement. The man hesitated, reluctant to let them in, but since Freddy's press card was perfectly legitimate, he decided not to argue and waved them through.

'Where do you suppose the plane is?' said Gertie, looking about her. 'I presume they don't leave them outside overnight.'

'It must be in one of these hangars,' said Freddy. He stopped a workman who happened to be passing. 'I say, could you tell us where the Nugent plane is?'

The workman looked at him blankly and walked on.

'Well, so much for that,' said Freddy.

'We'll just have to search for it ourselves, then,' said Gertie. Without further ado she set off towards the nearest hangar, ignoring the many curious looks from the people who were hurrying to and fro, preparing for that day's event. Freddy followed.

'Now, then, you can't go in there, young lady,' said a man whose peaked cap denoted his officialdom as they approached the hangar.

'I just want—' began Gertie, but the man was firm.

'Never mind what you just want. Nobody's allowed in. You can wait until the show starts, like everybody else.'

He shooed them away, and they retreated and considered their next move.

'How are Dauncey and Penbrigg going to get in if we can't?' said Gertie.

'Penbrigg's in the business,' said Freddy. 'Of course he'll be able to get in. And I dare say he'll be able to sneak Dauncey through easily enough.'

Gertie looked down at her gauzy evening-dress.

'I wish I'd put something else on before we set off. We're far too conspicuous in these clothes.' She glanced about anxiously. 'It's getting light now, and there are a lot more people about. If they're hoping to spirit the plane away without anybody seeing it they'll have to be quick.' She looked back at the first hangar. 'That man's gone. Let's try again.'

This time they got in easily enough, and found two aeroplanes inside, neither of which was the Nugent Nuthatch. A mechanic was tinkering with one of them. He looked up and spotted them.

'Public aren't allowed in here,' he said. 'Engineers only. Here, Bert, what are you doing letting the visitors in at this time?'

Bert turned out to be the man in the peaked cap who had shooed them away before.

'I thought I told you two to keep out,' he said crossly.

He squinted at them more closely and evidently came to the conclusion that there was something suspicious about them.

'Did you let these two in?' he said to a man who was approaching. They recognized him as the official who had let them through when they arrived.

'Yes—they said they was press, but now I'm not so sure,' replied the other man, looking them up and down.

Freddy decided it was time to come clean.

'Look here, I really am press,' he said, 'but that's not exactly why we're here. We've had word that someone is going to try and steal one of the planes today, and we've come to stop it.'

'Get away with you,' said Bert disbelievingly. Then a look of understanding dawned over his face, and his manner became slightly more sympathetic. 'Why don't you go home and sleep it off, there's a good fellow, then come back later. And you, miss. Does your mother know where you are?'

'No, she doesn't, as a matter of fact,' said Gertie, struck. 'Bother! Oh, never mind, she ought to know me well enough by now.'

'We really haven't been drinking,' said Freddy. 'At least, not for the last few hours,' he added honestly. 'And I wasn't joking about the plane. There are two dangerous men somewhere around here—one of them is a murderer—and they're going to take the Nugent Nuthatch.'

'Well, if that's true don't you worry,' said the gate-keeper soothingly. 'We'll keep an eye on things for you and make sure everything is safe. Now, you just get back in your car and go home. The show starts at ten o'clock and you'll feel all the better for a few hours' sleep.'

He and Bert escorted them firmly back to the car, and they had no choice but to get in and drive away.

'We can't leave now!' exclaimed Gertie, looking back as the aerodrome buildings retreated into the distance behind them.

'We're not leaving,' said Freddy. He drove a little way further until they were out of sight, then drew the car over to the grass verge and stopped. 'We'll just have to walk, that's all. It's not far over the fields.'

They alighted from the car and walked back, using trees and hedgerows as cover where possible, for it was getting lighter by the minute. This time they took a circuitous route, avoiding the main building.

'Let's start from the farthest hangar,' said Freddy. They crept behind a little cluster of huts and peeped out. Here several aeroplanes had already been brought out of their hangars. At first they did not see the Nuthatch, then Gertie jumped and clutched at Freddy's arm.

'Look!' she whispered.

Two men had emerged from the end hangar, wheeling a sleek aeroplane between them.

'It's the Nuthatch!' said Freddy.

Penbrigg and Dauncey had changed into workmen's clothes, and looked exactly like all the other mechanics in the place, except that they were carrying pilot's helmets. Nobody was giving them a second glance. They brought the plane down to the end of the runway, and Dauncey placed chocks under the wheels while Penbrigg climbed onto the wing, then got in and strapped on his helmet. Still nobody was paying them any attention. Dauncey, too, climbed in and started the engine. Then he climbed out again, examined a cable and adjusted something.

'We must stop them!' said Gertie.

She ran out from behind the hut and towards the Nuthatch, followed by Freddy. There were shouts, and Bert appeared again.

'Oi! I thought I told you—' he began.

Gertie dodged him adroitly and kept on running. Bert followed. Dauncey saw that they had been spotted.

'Keep back!' he said. He took out the gun and levelled it at Bert, who stopped.

'Here, what's all this, then?' he said, but retreated.

'Gertie!' said Freddy.

But Gertie was not listening. She slowed, eyeing the gun warily, but walked straight up to Dauncey, who gave her a cheerful smile quite in the ordinary way.

'Hallo, Gertie, come to see us off?' he said.

'He killed Doug, and you're going to let him escape,' she said sorrowfully.

'I have no choice,' he said.

He was standing straight, and the early light softened his worn look. At that moment he appeared something like the handsome hero he had once been. Then his mouth twisted ruefully.

'Cheer up, Gertie!' he said. 'You never know—perhaps I'll redeem myself one day.'

He knocked the chocks away, then climbed into the plane and adjusted a dial or two, and they watched as it taxied slowly down the runway, then gathered speed and took off smoothly into the grey dawn.

'Too late!' said Gertie tragically, as Freddy came to stand beside her.

They watched as the plane got smaller and smaller. It was already over the sea now, climbing higher and higher into the sky—higher than it possibly needed to, surely.

'What the devil's he doing?' said Freddy suddenly.

The plane was no longer receding into the distance, but had levelled off and turned. Now it seemed to slow almost to a stop. A finger of sunlight appeared over the horizon and glinted off its wings. The Nuthatch hovered for what seemed like an age, then they watched, aghast, as its nose tipped slowly and it began to fall freely. Down, down, down it came, spiralling, plummeting towards the sea, until it was out of sight. There was no sound as it hit the sea. There were cries of horror all around, and men began to run and shout instructions, but Freddy and Gertie did not move.

'He did it on purpose,' said Gertie at last.

'It looks like it,' said Freddy.

'Then he was a hero after all.'

'I suppose he was, in a manner of speaking,' said Freddy. He turned to Gertie. 'You look tired, old girl,' he said. 'Let's go home.'

CHAPTER TWENTY-FOUR

TWO WEEKS LATER Freddy went to tea with Lois Westray at the Georgian restaurant in Harrods again. She was dressed more soberly than usual, and was looking pale and careworn, but was doing her best to appear her usual self.

'It's been a bad couple of weeks, all told,' she said. 'We had no idea Leslie had been up to anything of the kind. He just didn't seem the type. And poor old Hector Finkley! He was a gentle soul—lived in his own little world, but terribly enthusiastic about his work, and only too glad to give a younger inventor a helping hand. And to think that's how he was repaid! It must have come as a terrible shock to him when he found out what Leslie was really like.'

'I don't suppose he had much time to think about it,' said Freddy. 'His death was quick, as I understand it. One hard shove and it was all over.'

She winced.

'And then for Leslie to run down poor, unsuspecting Mrs. Finkley, too—and she didn't even have anything to do with it!'

'Yes,' said Freddy. 'I feel rather bad about that. After all, he only did it because he thought she'd been telling me something that would compromise him—which, as it happens, she had, but if he'd left well alone and not tried to run me over I'd never have given the matter a second thought.'

'The police have been looking into Frank, by the way,' said Lois. 'It seems he wasn't quite as bad as he was made out to be. It all started a few years ago when he accidentally passed on some information to Salmanov which seemed unimportant at the time. He wasn't paid for it, or anything—just let it slip in conversation, as anyone might. But after that, Salmanov threatened to expose him for that mistake if he didn't keep on doing it, so he felt forced to go along with it. It was weakness rather than dishonesty for the most part. He was terribly weak in some ways, but terribly brave in others. He really did deserve his reputation as a war hero. It's just a shame it all went wrong afterwards.'

Freddy thought that Lois was trying to convince herself that Dauncey had not been as dishonest as he had seemed. He did not quite agree, but said nothing. If that was what she wanted to believe then who was he to stop her?

'Well, he did redeem himself in the end,' he said. 'He could have shot us at any time, you know. Penbrigg certainly wanted to, but Dauncey got the gun off him and, I think, saved our lives deliberately. I shall always be grateful to him for that.'

'I'm glad.' She gave him a sad little smile, then said briskly, 'By the way, I've confessed to Stanley about the wing slot plans and thrown myself on his mercy.'

'Good Lord! How did he take it?'

She threw him a wry look.

'Not too well, as you can imagine, but I hope he'll forgive me. He's upset about lots of other things at the moment, and I mean to be awfully good to him and look after him. The whole business with Doug has upset him dreadfully, especially since it turned out it wasn't suicide at all. But one good thing has come out of it at least: it seems Walter had no idea that Nugent Corporation had won the Woodville Prize from a stolen design, so he came to visit the other day and beg pardon. Then Stanley begged pardon in turn for what happened to the Nuthatch, and then they got talking and found they have more in common than they thought. Stanley brought out Finkley's old notebook, and when I left them they'd put their heads together and were talking about forming a partnership to develop some of Finkley's ideas.'

'That sounds like a splendid plan.'

'Yes,' she said. 'It's just a pity Finkley won't be here to see them.'

Everything about this case was a pity, Freddy thought. His next stop was Badenoch House. Lady Browncliffe and Tatty were in. Lady Browncliffe stayed to talk for a few minutes, then went off to speak to Sally about something. Tatty was also putting a brave face on things. She remarked brightly on Freddy's recent adventure, and was careful to say that she had read about it in the *Clarion*, then went on:

'Did you know Tom and Irene got married yesterday? His father isn't happy at all, but Tom doesn't care, he says. They're going out to Kenya to take up farming.'

'Is that so? Ah, yes, I seem to remember he mentioned something of the sort, once. I don't think he's very interested in aeroplanes.'

'No, he's not. He mentioned Kenya to me, too, and I didn't like the sound of it at all. But I don't need to worry about it now that he's married someone else. He came to apologize the other day, but I said it was quite all right and we'd rushed into it anyway and I wished him every happiness.'

'And do you?'

'Yes. It would have been a mistake to marry him when I was still thinking about Doug.' There were tears in her eyes. 'I miss Doug terribly, but it's been such a relief to have it proved that I didn't drive him to suicide. It would have been an awful burden of guilt to live with, and at least I can comfort myself with the thought that he died trying to do the right thing.'

'That's true enough. I'm only sorry I didn't see sooner that it was Penbrigg. I'd never noticed his ruthless streak before, although I really ought to have. After all, he broke enough of my things at school and never paid me back for them. Still, it wouldn't have helped Douglas. I suppose Alida must be upset, too, is she?'

'Oh, she's not too bad. She liked Leslie, but she found his shyness rather exasperating. She's a little down, but we're going to pick ourselves up and get on with things. Mother and Lois have been conspiring together and we're all going abroad for the winter—I don't know where. Somewhere a long way from machines and inventions and air shows, with lots of nice hotels and places to go dancing and enjoy oneself in the sunshine.'

'Well, I wish you the best of it,' he said.

He took his leave and went out, then glanced at his watch. It was a quarter to six, and London glowed warm in the evening sunshine. He strolled the mile or so to Grosvenor Square and stood at the corner, leaning against a lamp-post and smoking. At length he saw a figure approaching. Gertie was looking very pretty in a flower-patterned frock, and she flashed him a mischievous grin as she arrived.

'Give me a cigarette, will you?' she said. 'I've been gasping for one all day.'

Freddy supplied her with the requested article and lit it for her.

'Have they given you your latch-key back yet?' he said.

'No such luck! I've had to promise to be back by ten,' she said gloomily. 'It's too bad, being a woman. I'll bet nobody's ever threatened to stop *your* allowance for staying out all night. I pointed out that I'd been doing my civic duty and catching a murderer, but it cut no ice at all. They said I wasn't to be trusted, which is rot, of course. By the way, you'd better not tell Father I'm meeting you. He thinks you're a bad influence on me.'

'*I'm* a bad influence on *you?* That's rich! I should rather say it was the other way round.'

'Nonsense. I am a paragon of good behaviour at all times. Now, where can we go and get a drink? I haven't had a cocktail in two weeks at least.'

'Plenty of time for that later. Let's go for a walk,' said Freddy.

They headed for Hyde Park and walked as far as the bandstand, where a brass band was just concluding an afternoon concert. They stood among the crowd and watched, then Freddy became aware of a familiar presence at his shoulder, and turned to see Corky Beckwith, wearing his usual ingratiating smile.

'Is there to be no peace?' said Freddy wearily.

'Can't a man watch a public performance of music without being harangued?' said Corky, affecting an expression of deep hurt. 'After a day spent in dauntless battle with the intricacies of the English language and those who would seek to shun the light of truth, one wants nothing more than to allow the dulcet notes of the slide trombone to drift gently into one's consciousness, and yet all you do is hurl unwarranted abuse at me.'

'Rot,' said Freddy.

'Evidently its charms haven't soothed *your* savage breast, at any rate,' said Corky.

'Can't you just leave us alone? The story's over and done with, we brought your car back in perfect condition, and there's nothing else we have to say that you could possibly be interested in.'

'Hmph. Think yourself lucky I didn't have you charged with theft. But as a matter of fact, the car episode fitted in perfectly with my story. You know, plucky reporter wins over against overwhelming odds, and all that.'

'Ah yes, that sensational work of fiction you published in which you turned up, wrestled heroically with the would-be murderers and saved my life and the life of the helpless Lady Gertrude McAloon.'

'Well, what of it?' said Corky, as Gertie snorted at the very idea of being considered helpless.

'That's not how *I* remember it happening. As I recall, Dauncey hauled you in then clipped you one over the ear and made you cry like a girl.'

'Your memory fails you once again, young Freddy. And anyway, I still beat you to the original Dauncey story.'

'Oh, stop it,' said Gertie, seeing that they were about to begin bickering interminably. She tugged at Freddy's arm. 'Come on—it's too nice an evening for this sort of thing. Let's leave him to his savage trombone, or whatever it is.'

They wandered off and down a path towards the Serpentine. The grass was parched and yellow after the hot summer, but the trees were lush and green, and there was the scent of flowers in the air. People were walking to and fro, enjoying the warmth of the evening, and the sounds of the city could be heard in the distance. They found a bench by the Serpentine and sat down. Freddy was not the sort of man to look too far ahead, but Gertie was good company and he was enjoying being with her for the moment. They talked for a while, then she looked up at him and smiled, and he put his arm round her and kissed her. It was all very easy and pleasant.

'Look here, I have a deadline to meet. Are you engaged or not?' said a voice just behind them. It was Corky.

Freddy raised his eyes to heaven. Gertie giggled and turned.

'Not yet, but you never know!' she said.

New Releases

If you'd like to receive news of further releases by Clara Benson, you can sign up to my mailing list here.

CLARABENSON.COM/NEWSLETTER

Or follow me on Facebook.

FACEBOOK.COM/CLARABENSONBOOKS

New to Freddy? Read more about him in the Angela Marchmont mysteries.

ClaraBenson.com/books

Books in This Series

- A Case of Blackmail in Belgravia
- A Case of Murder in Mayfair
- A Case of Conspiracy in Clerkenwell
- A Case of Duplicity in Dorset
- A Case of Suicide in St. James's

Also by Clara Benson:

The Angela Marchmont Mysteries

Made in the USA
San Bernardino,
CA

58982101R00163